EBONVALE : SHADOWS OF SECRETS

AF581963

UTAKARSH SINGH

Copyright © Utakarsh Singh
All Rights Reserved.

This book has been self-published with all reasonable efforts taken to make the material error-free by the author. No part of this book shall be used, reproduced in any manner whatsoever without written permission from the author, except in the case of brief quotations embodied in critical articles and reviews.

The Author of this book is solely responsible and liable for its content including but not limited to the views, representations, descriptions, statements, information, opinions and references ["Content"]. The Content of this book shall not constitute or be construed or deemed to reflect the opinion or expression of the Publisher or Editor. Neither the Publisher nor Editor endorse or approve the Content of this book or guarantee the reliability, accuracy or completeness of the Content published herein and do not make any representations or warranties of any kind, express or implied, including but not limited to the implied warranties of merchantability, fitness for a particular purpose. The Publisher and Editor shall not be liable whatsoever for any errors, omissions, whether such errors or omissions result from negligence, accident, or any other cause or claims for loss or damages of any kind, including without limitation, indirect or consequential loss or damage arising out of use, inability to use, or about the reliability, accuracy or sufficiency of the information contained in this book.

Made with ♥ on the Notion Press Platform
www.notionpress.com

To my family—your unwavering support and love have been the foundation on which I've built not only this story but every step of my life. You've embraced my wild ideas and endless nights of writing, and for that, I am forever grateful. This book is a testament to the strength of our bond.

To my friends—you've been my sounding boards, my motivators, and the ones who pulled me out of my own shadows when I needed it most. Your belief in me has meant the world, and this journey wouldn't have been the same without your constant encouragement and positivity.

And to my father—your faith in me has never faltered, even when mine did. You've been my inspiration, my guide, and my greatest champion. This story of darkness and secrets could only have been written with the light you've always brought into my life. Thank you for always encouraging me to chase my dreams, no matter how distant they seemed.

Contents

Foreword *vii*

Preface *ix*

Acknowledgements *xi*

Prologue *xiii*

1. Shadows Of The Thicket 1
2. Ebonvale's Whispering Shadows 9
3. Misttvale Crossing - The Real Mystery Begins 16
4. Echoes Beneath The Lanterns 21
5. Veil Of Dread 28
6. Echoing Hollow: The New Mystery 33
7. Echoing Hollow: Beyond Misttvale Crossing 36
8. Echoing Hollow: The Forgotten Dead 41
9. Echoing Hollow: Into The Heart Of Darkness 46
10. The Forsaken Hall's Horrors 51
11. Echoing Hollow's Hidden Curse 55
12. Shadows Of The Forsaken Woods 59
13. The Vanishing Of Finnian 65
14. The Grave Of Shadows 69
15. Footsteps To The Unknown 73
16. The Mayor's Deceit: The Coal Conspiracy 77
17. The Coal Conspiracy: Unravelling Ebonvale's Darkness 85
18. Fading Shadows: Ebonvale's Redemption Unveiled 92

Part 1

Epilogue 103

Author's Note 105

Foreword

In a world where shadows stretch long and the echoes of the past resonate with the present, Ebonvale: Shadows of Secrets draws readers into a hauntingly captivating tale. The author has woven a rich tapestry of suspense, mystery, and supernatural elements that grip the imagination from the very first page.

Set against the backdrop of Ebonvale, a village steeped in darkness and secrets, this story follows Cyrus, Finnian, Evelyn, and Jake as they navigate the treacherous waters of friendship and fear. The author brilliantly captures the essence of a small town where every corner may hide a lurking danger, and every whisper carries a weighty secret.

This book is a testament to the author's creativity and their ability to conjure a chilling atmosphere that lingers long after the last page is turned. Prepare to lose yourself in a world where the line between the living and the dead is blurred, and where the quest for truth reveals the darkest corners of human nature.

As you embark on this journey through Ebonvale, remember: some secrets are meant to stay buried

Preface

Welcome to Ebonvale—a village where shadows whisper, the past is never truly buried, and every lantern flickers with a hidden secret. As you turn these pages, you'll be joining Cyrus, Finnian, Evelyn, and Jake on a journey into a place haunted not only by ghosts but by the weight of unsolved mysteries and forgotten sins.

The idea for Ebonvale: Shadows of Secrets began as a spark, a faint whisper from a world I could only imagine. I've always been drawn to tales of the unknown, stories where the line between the living and the dead is blurred, where the past bleeds into the present in unsettling ways. But more than that, I wanted to create a mystery that digs deep into the human psyche—the fear of what's hiding in the shadows, and the secrets we all carry.

The journey of writing this story has been one of discovery, both for my characters and myself. With every twist and turn, I found myself lost in the eerie atmosphere of Ebonvale, a place where nothing is as it seems, and even the most trusted faces can hide terrifying truths.

But this book is not just about fear—it's about bravery, friendship, and the relentless pursuit of truth. As you join Cyrus, Finnian, Evelyn, Jake, and their companions in uncovering the dark secrets of their village, I hope you'll feel the same tension and curiosity that gripped me as I wrote it.

This story is my attempt to capture that elusive feeling we all know—the chill that creeps up our spine when we sense something is not quite right, the fleeting glance of movement in the corner of our eye when no one is there. It's a reminder that the scariest things in life are often not the ones we can see, but the ones we can only feel.

To those who have supported me along this path—my family, friends, and especially my dad—thank you for being my guiding lights in the darkness. Your encouragement has helped turn this dream into reality.

As you turn these pages, prepare yourself for a descent into mystery and fear. The shadows of Ebonvale are alive, and they have stories to tell—if you dare to listen.

So, dear reader, step carefully into Ebonvale. The secrets here are waiting to be uncovered... but be warned—once you step into the shadows, there's no turning back.

Acknowledgements

Writing this book has been an incredible journey, and there are many people I would like to thank for their support and encouragement along the way.

First and foremost, I want to express my heartfelt gratitude to my family. Your unwavering belief in my dreams has inspired me to push through every challenge I faced while crafting this story. To my dad, thank you for your constant encouragement and for instilling in me a love for storytelling. Your support means the world to me.

To my friends, who cheered me on, listened to my ideas, and provided invaluable feedback, thank you for being my sounding board and my greatest supporters. Each of you has played a crucial role in shaping this book, and I am so grateful for your enthusiasm and insights.

I would also like to acknowledge my writing group and mentors, whose guidance has been instrumental in my growth as a writer. Your constructive critiques and encouragement have helped me refine my craft and push the boundaries of my imagination.

To the readers—thank you for choosing to embark on this journey through Ebonvale. Your willingness to step into the shadows and explore the mysteries within these pages is what makes this all worthwhile.

Lastly, I want to thank the countless storytellers who have come before me, whose tales of horror and mystery have inspired me to weave my own narrative. Your creativity and passion continue to light the way for aspiring writers everywhere.

As you dive into the depths of Ebonvale, I hope you find as much joy in reading this story as I found in writing it and enjoy this exploration of fear, friendship, and the unrelenting quest for truth. May the shadows whisper their secrets to you. Welcome to the Ebonvale.

Prologue

In the heart of a forgotten realm, shrouded in a veil of perpetual mist, lies the village of Ebonvale—a place where time seems to stand still, and the air thickens with whispers of the damned. Here, shadows twist and writhe as if alive, dancing to the haunting melody of lost souls who wander the cobblestone streets long after dusk has fallen. Lanterns flicker nervously, their feeble light barely piercing the dark, as if aware of the secrets lurking in the depths of the night.

Once a vibrant community, Ebonvale now bears the scars of its haunted history, a tapestry woven with sorrow and despair. The villagers, with hollow eyes and trembling hands, walk the streets in silence, casting wary glances over their shoulders as if they feel the cold breath of the past lingering just behind them. A suffocating dread blankets the village, wrapping its inhabitants in a shroud of fear that tightens with each passing day.

Among the legends that echo through the fog, several stand out—tales of Misttvale Crossing, where shadows whisper secrets of lost souls; the cursed valley of Echoing Hollow, which consumes those who dare to enter its depths; and the dark embrace of Forsaken Woods, a forest steeped in mystery and dread. Whispers tell of twisted spirits and malevolent forces, where the veil between the living and the dead is perilously thin. The ominous Blackwater Lake, abandoned and shunned, mirrors the darkness of the past, reflecting the haunting of Echoing Hollow and the tragedies that haunt Forsaken Hall, the old Town Hall of the village. As the Lantern Festival approaches, a sinister darkness begins to unfurl like a phantom, creeping into the hearts of the unsuspecting, drawing them closer to the horrors that lie within.

On a night when the moon's light falters and shadows deepen, four friends—Cyrus, Finnian, Evelyn, and Jake—are drawn together by fate, their bonds tested as they step into the encroaching darkness. With courage ignited by the flame of curiosity, they embark on a quest for truth, unaware that the secrets they seek are not merely remnants of the past, but living entities that yearn for release.

As they navigate the treacherous landscape of Ebonvale, they find themselves haunted by specters of the unknown—echoes of those who vanished without a trace, their pleas for justice mingling with the cries of the wind. Every shadow carries a story, every corner conceals a horror, and with each heartbeat, the tension mounts, threatening to unravel the very fabric of their reality.

In this forsaken village, the past is not dead; it lurks in the corners, waiting for the unwary to stumble upon its hidden truths. The friends will soon learn that some secrets are forged in darkness, and the shadows hold far more than they could ever imagine.

Welcome to Ebonvale, where every flickering lantern reveals another layer of fear, and the echoes of the lost call out for those brave enough to listen.

CHAPTER ONE

Shadows of the Thicket

Cyrus Dusk stood at the edge of Ebonvale, his heart pounding as the fog began to roll in from the thicket, swallowing the village in a dense veil of Gray. It was that time of year again—the time when the shadows lengthened and the air grew heavy with secrets. He could feel it in his bones, a familiar chill that crept up his spine every autumn, whispering of things best left undisturbed.

The Lantern Festival was meant to be a time of celebration, but for Cyrus, it always brought a deep unease. The fog that crept in from the thicket wasn't just mist; it carried the weight of his family's grief—an unsolved mystery that still haunted Ebonvale. Eighteen years ago, his uncle, Alfred Dusk, had vanished without a trace during the festival. Cyrus had been too young to understand it then, but now, every time the mist returned, so did the memories.

His father had told him that Alfred had wandered into the thicket, drawn by the strange lights and shadows that danced in the fog. It was said that the Lantern Festival was cursed—an omen that heralded the shadows' return. Cyrus clenched his fists, staring into the thickening mist, as if hoping to glimpse the truth that had eluded them for so long. Eighteen years had passed, but not a day went by that he didn't think of his uncle—of how the festival had stolen him away, just as it had countless others over the years.

"I'll find you, Uncle Alfred," Cyrus whispered to himself, his voice barely audible over the rustling of the wind. A fierce determination burned within him. He would uncover the truth, no matter what it cost him. This festival, this year—it would be different. He would not let the shadows claim anyone else, especially not Finnian.

A noise stirred behind him, and Cyrus's mind snapped back to the present. The fog had thickened around him, swallowing the village in its eerie embrace. His eyes darted around, searching for his brother.

"Cyrus! Come on!" Finnian's voice broke through the gloom, cheerful and carefree as he darted past, his silhouette a fleeting shadow against the encroaching fog. The younger brother's laughter echoed, a sound that felt almost out of place amid the growing darkness. "You're going to miss it!"

Cyrus hesitated, glancing back at the village behind him. The townsfolk were gathering in the square for the annual Lantern Festival, a celebration of light that masked the deeper fears of Ebonvale. But Cyrus felt drawn to the thicket, where the real mysteries of their town lay hidden. He knew he should join Finnian, but the fog always seemed to beckon him, whispering promises of forgotten tales.

"You can't let the fog scare you!" Finnian shouted, his voice a mixture of challenge and excitement. "It's just a bunch of shadows! Come on!"

With a resigned sigh, Cyrus pushed his doubts aside and followed, but a nagging feeling remained in the back of his mind. The shadows in the thicket were different this year, thicker, almost sentient, swirling in a way that felt alive. As they reached the village square, lanterns flickered to life, casting a warm glow that fought back the darkness. But beyond the glow, the thicket loomed, dark and silent, hiding secrets that had been buried for too long.

Cyrus watched as Finnian darted toward the festivities, but his gaze lingered on the edges of the fog, where shadows seemed to dance just out of sight. He couldn't shake the feeling that the fog had something to say, that it was more than just a seasonal occurrence. And as the night unfolded, he couldn't help but wonder what secrets it would reveal—secrets that would change everything for him and Finnian.

Thinking all these while walking, he suddenly felt something. Something that was enough for Cyrus to make his moves faster. He held the hand of Finnian and started walking faster. Faster as much as he can. "What happened Cyrus? Why are you walking so fast" Finnian asked. But Cyrus was not in the state of mind that he could explain that situation to Finnian.

Cyrus tightened his grip on Finnian's hand, urging him to keep pace as they navigated through the village square. The cheerful laughter and music from the Lantern Festival faded into a distant murmur, overshadowed by a growing sense of unease.

"Cyrus, seriously! What's going on?" Finnian insisted, glancing up at his brother with a mixture of confusion and concern.

"I... I don't know," Cyrus replied, his voice low and urgent. "But something feels off. The shadows... they're moving differently tonight."

Finnian's brows furrowed, his youthful bravado faltering for a moment. "You're just imagining things. It's probably just the fog. Come on, let's enjoy the festival!"

But Cyrus couldn't shake the feeling that they weren't alone. The fog felt thicker, almost oppressive, and the shadows around them seemed to flicker with an unsettling life of their own. He could swear he saw them darting between the lanterns, whispering secrets he couldn't quite hear.

As they reached the edge of the square, a chilling wind swept through, extinguishing several lanterns in a heartbeat. The laughter turned into gasps, and the once-bright square dimmed ominously.

"Cyrus!" Finnian called, panic creeping into his voice.

Suddenly, from the direction of the thicket, a shadow separated itself from the darkness, elongating and twisting unnaturally as it moved toward them. Cyrus felt a primal instinct kick in—a desperate need to protect his brother.

"Run!" he shouted, pulling Finnian along. They dashed through the crowd, dodging startled festival-goers, the festive atmosphere now replaced by confusion and fear.

They veered into an alley that led toward the thicket, where the shadows were thickest. Cyrus could feel his heart racing as the whispers grew louder, a chorus of voices rising in intensity.

"What is that? What's happening?" Finnian gasped, struggling to keep up.

"I don't know!" Cyrus replied, adrenaline coursing through him. "But we need to find a safe place!"

As they reached the thicket, the shadows seemed to reach out toward them, brushing against their skin like cold fingers. Cyrus spotted a small clearing where the trees parted slightly, the fog swirling more violently around the edges.

"In there!" he urged, and they plunged into the clearing, the shadows closing in behind them. "What's going on, Cyrus? Why are we running?" Finnian panted, trying to keep up.

"I don't have time to explain everything right now," Cyrus replied, his voice tense. "We just need to stick together and find Grayson." He kept his head low as they squeezed through the narrow clearing, the branches above them looming like dark sentinels.

Suddenly, the air around them grew heavy, and an unnatural chill seeped into their bones. The shadows seemed to thicken, twisting and coiling as if alive, and Cyrus could hear the faintest of whispers weaving through the fog.

As they emerged from the narrow path, they stumbled into a larger clearing dominated by a towering tree, its gnarled roots twisting like skeletal hands clutching the earth. At its base, they found Old Man Grayson, sitting cross-legged and eerily calm amidst the chaos around them.

"You've come," he said, his voice a raspy whisper that somehow carried over the sound of the rustling leaves. "The shadows have awakened, and they're hungry for the truth."

Cyrus felt a surge of urgency. "Grayson, what's happening? Why are the shadows after us?"

Grayson's eyes, clouded yet piercing, seemed to look straight through Cyrus. "The fog is a barrier, protecting the town from the shadows' true nature. But once it thickens, it awakens the spirits bound to this land. They are drawn to those who seek answers, and they will stop at nothing to keep their secrets hidden."

Finnian, wide-eyed and trembling, whispered, "What do we do?"

"You must confront the shadows," Grayson said, raising a hand to silence them. "Only by facing what lies within can you uncover the truth about Ebonvale. But beware—the shadows reflect your deepest fears."

"Shouldn't we tell Jake about all this, Cyrus?" Finnian asked, glancing nervously around the clearing.

"We should," Cyrus replied, his brow furrowed in thought. "But first, I think we need to talk to Evelyn. She can help us more, especially after what happened during the last year's festival."

"What incident? You didn't mention anything about that," Finnian pressed, his curiosity piqued.

"She saw the ghost of Victor Valtor," Cyrus explained, his voice low. "You know who Victor Valtor is, right?"

Finnian's eyes widened in realization. "Victor Valtor? The one who disappeared during the first Lantern Festival? They say he haunts the thicket!"

Cyrus nodded gravely. "Exactly. If Evelyn encountered him, she might have valuable insights about the shadows we're facing."

Suddenly, a rustle in the nearby bushes made both brothers jump. A figure stepped into the clearing, and it was Evelyn, her face pale but determined.

“I was looking for you two!” she exclaimed, her voice shaky yet resolute. “I heard what happened at the festival, and I felt... something was wrong. The shadows—they’re changing. They’re more aggressive.”

“Evelyn,” Cyrus said urgently, “we need to know what you saw during the festival. It could be the key to understanding what’s happening now.”

Evelyn hesitated, glancing around as if the shadows themselves might be listening. “During the festival, I saw him—Victor. He was trying to warn me about something. But then the fog rolled in, and I couldn’t hear him clearly.”

Cyrus exchanged a look with Finnian. “We have to find out what he wanted to tell you. It might help us confront the shadows.”

“But how?” Finnian asked. “What if we can’t face them?”

“We will face them together,” Cyrus assured them. “Evelyn, do you remember any specific details? Anything about what Victor tried to show you?”

Evelyn closed her eyes, trying to recall the vision. “There was a symbol—a mark on a tree near the thicket. I think it was important. It felt like... like it was calling to me.”

“Then we should go check that mark,” Cyrus said. “Maybe it can help us solve the mystery of Victor’s warning.”

Evelyn nodded in agreement, but Finnian’s gaze remained fixed on the thicket, his expression a mix of shock and fear. Cyrus could sense his brother’s unease and made a decision.

“I think you’ll be safer here with Grayson, Finnian,” Cyrus said gently. “We’ll just go to find Jake, and then we’ll look for that tree. You can stay here with the old man until we get back.”

Finnian opened his mouth to protest, but Cyrus raised a hand. “I need you to trust me. We’ll be quick, and we won’t take any chances. Just wait for us.”

Reluctantly, Finnian nodded, though the worry in his eyes didn’t fade.

"Be careful," he whispered, his voice barely audible as they turned to leave.

As they made their way through the fog, Cyrus and Evelyn reached the village square where they last saw Jake. The air felt thick with tension, and the shadows seemed to cling to their heels.

"Where do you think Jake went?" Evelyn asked, scanning the area.

"He was sceptical about the festival. He might have gone home," Cyrus replied, his eyes darting around. "Let's check there first."

When they arrived at Jake's house, they spotted him standing outside, looking troubled. Relief washed over his face as he saw them.

"Cyrus! Evelyn!" Jake called, waving them over. "I was just about to look for you. Things got really strange after you left."

Cyrus wasted no time. "We need your help. Evelyn saw Victor Valtor's ghost last year during the festival, and we think we've found a clue connected to his warning."

Jake raised an eyebrow. "Victor? The ghost everyone talks about? You can't be serious."

"I am," Evelyn interjected, urgency in her tone. "We need to check a mark on a tree in the thicket that might be important. Will you come with us?"

Jake hesitated, his scepticism battling with concern for his friends. "I don't know, guys. This all sounds... insane."

"It might be our only chance to uncover the truth," Cyrus insisted, desperation creeping into his voice. "We're already in deep. We need you with us."

After a moment of contemplation, Jake sighed. "Alright, I'll go. But if anything happens—"

"We'll stick together," Cyrus assured him. "Just like we always do."

"Okay, as you say," Evelyn replied, her voice steady despite the growing unease. The trio, hearts filled with a mix of courage and

fear, stepped into the thick fog of the thicket.

CHAPTER TWO

Ebonvale's Whispering Shadows

Ebonvale was a village shrouded in mystery, but it was also a beautiful place. Lakes shimmered under the sunlight, bridges arched gracefully over quiet streams, and valleys rolled into a small forest known as the Forsaken Woods. This lush woodland stood just behind the thicket, perpetually wrapped in a blanket of fog. Their first real challenge was Misttvale Crossing, a picturesque yet foreboding area.

The villagers whispered about Misttvale. It was a place of stunning beauty, but also of unspeakable horror. Years ago, a group of tourists vanished without a trace, swallowed by the mist. Victor Valtor had been one of them, but unlike the others, he had somehow managed to escape. Yet whatever he had witnessed there shattered his sanity, and the following year during the Lantern Festival, he himself disappeared from the thicket, never to be seen again.

Evelyn remembered the shadowy figure she had seen last year—Victor's ghost. She didn't recognize him at first, but the villagers and Old Man Grayson described the tattered clothing and shabby hat Victor had worn the day he disappeared, and it was exactly what the apparition had been wearing.

The fog pressed in around them now, dense and suffocating. They carried a single lantern, its flickering light barely cutting through the thick mist. Their footsteps quickened as they navigated the twisting paths of the thicket. And then, suddenly a sudden chill swept through the air, more frigid than the surrounding fog, and the lantern's flame flickered violently. Evelyn stopped in her tracks; her eyes wide with fear. "Did you feel that?" she whispered.

Before Cyrus could respond, the light in the lantern sputtered and went out, plunging them into darkness. A cold, suffocating silence fell over the thicket, broken only by the faint rustling of leaves. Then, from the shadows, they heard it—a soft, almost imperceptible whisper, like the distant echoes of voices long lost.

Jake turned toward the sound, his face pale. "What... what was that?"

The whispers grew louder, swirling around them, and Cyrus strained to make out the words. But they were incoherent, fragmented, as if the voices were trapped between worlds.

"Don't listen to them," Evelyn said sharply, her voice trembling. "That's how it started last time. That's how he—Victor—appeared."

A sudden rustling in the bushes made them all jump. From the corner of his eye, Cyrus caught movement—something shifting in the fog. A shadowy figure, barely visible, was watching them from the edge of the trees. It was tall and gaunt, its shape distorted by the mist.

"Who's there?" Cyrus called out, his voice steady despite the panic rising in his chest.

The figure didn't move. It just stood there, motionless, its head slightly tilted as if observing them. Then, without a sound, it began to glide toward them—slow, deliberate, almost inhuman in its movements.

"Run!" Evelyn shouted, grabbing the lantern and bolting in the opposite direction. Cyrus and Jake followed, their hearts pounding in their ears as they raced through the thickening fog. The path twisted beneath their feet, the trees closing in on them as if the forest itself was alive, trying to swallow them whole.

But the shadow was faster. They could hear it behind them, a scraping, dragging sound that seemed to grow closer with every step. Cyrus glanced back over his shoulder and saw the shadow looming larger, its distorted form stretching unnaturally toward them.

"We can't outrun it!" Jake shouted, panic seeping into his voice.

Ahead, the path split into two. Without thinking, Cyrus veered left, leading the others into a darker, narrower passageway. The air grew colder, and the fog thicker. Shadows flitted between the trees, some too quick to be human.

Then, they saw it. At the end of the path, barely visible through the mist, was a massive tree, its bark twisted and blackened as if it had been burned long ago. Carved into the trunk was a strange symbol—a symbol Evelyn recognized from her vision.

"That's it," she gasped. "That's the mark Victor showed me."

But as they neared the tree, the shadowy figure appeared again, this time directly in their path. It stood between them and the tree, its form flickering like a dying flame, and its face—what little they could see—was hollow, as if something had eaten away at its very essence.

The shadowy figure looming before them was a grotesque distortion of human form, but far from any living being. Its body was impossibly tall and gaunt, stretched thin as though drained of life. The edges of its silhouette flickered and shifted, never staying still, as though the fog itself was trying to swallow it whole.

Its skin, if it could be called that, was a mottled shade of ashen Gray, translucent in places, revealing the suggestion of bones beneath. Its long, spindly limbs hung loosely at its sides, swaying ever so slightly as if caught in a phantom breeze. The fingers, unnaturally long, ended in sharpened points that scraped softly against the ground as it moved, leaving shallow, jagged marks in the dirt.

The head was the most unsettling. It was tilted at an unnatural angle, as though the neck had been broken, and from within the hollow cavity of what should have been a face, an eerie glow pulsed faintly. No eyes, no mouth—just an empty, gaping void that seemed to suck in the surrounding light. Faint, ghostly whispers emanated from the figure, as if it carried the voices of lost souls, their words fragmented and barely audible, drowning in the thick fog.

Every breath the trio took was heavy, the air around them thickening like invisible hands pressing against their chests. The temperature plummeted, sending chills down their spines. It wasn't just cold—it was the kind of unnatural, bone-deep cold that came from the presence of something that didn't belong to the world of the living.

As the figure drew closer, the whispers grew louder, rising in intensity, though no distinct words could be made out. It was like a chorus of tormented souls, each voice overlapping the other, their anguish filling the night air. The lantern's light flickered weakly, struggling to push back the suffocating darkness that seemed to close in tighter with every passing second.

A faint, metallic scent filled the air—like rusted iron, sharp and unsettling—accompanied by the oppressive weight of dread. The atmosphere itself seemed to warp around the figure, the fog swirling with an unnatural life, its movement synchronized with the entity's slow, deliberate steps. The longer they stared at it, the more the world around them seemed to fade, as if the figure was pulling them into a place where reality itself unraveled.

The whispers surged around them, louder now, almost deafening. Cyrus could feel the pressure in his ears, the voices trying to burrow into his mind.

"What do we do?" Jake asked, his voice shaking.

Evelyn stepped forward; her eyes fixed on the shadow. "We have to face it. The truth is buried here, and it won't stop until we confront it."

Cyrus tightened his grip on the lantern, the cold seeping into his bones. "Then let's finish this."

Cyrus, adrenaline surging through his veins, hurled the lantern straight at the shadowy figure. But instead of making contact, the light passed right through its form as if it were nothing more than smoke. The figure barely flinched, but something terrifying happened—its outline grew sharper, the shadow revealing more of its ghastly, grotesque features. Its hollow face twisted into something resembling a grin, a mockery of human expression, as if mocking their attempts to fight back.

Evelyn's breath caught in her throat as she stared in horror. And then, like a spark igniting her memory, she suddenly remembered.

"Misttvale Crossing!" she shouted, her voice trembling but determined. "That's what Victor said to me! We have to go there, now!"

"Misttvale?" Jake's voice was tight with fear, his eyes never leaving the figure that now seemed to tower over them, tendrils of shadow twisting and reaching out like claws. "But what about the tree? The mark? What if it's our only clue?"

Cyrus glanced at the twisted bark of the tree and then back at the monstrous shadow, whose presence seemed to distort the air itself. The whispers had grown louder, more insistent, and the figure was closing in. Every second they lingered felt like a countdown to death.

"We'll come back for it!" Cyrus snapped, grabbing Jake's arm and pulling him back. "But if we stay here, we're dead. Running is our only chance!"

The shadow loomed closer, its long, spindly fingers reaching out as if to grasp them. The fog thickened, and the temperature around them dropped even further, making it feel like they were sinking into a frozen nightmare.

"Now!" Cyrus barked, and they all turned, sprinting into the fog.

Without daring to look behind them, the trio ran as fast as their legs could carry them, hearts pounding in their chests like war drums. The fog felt suffocating, thick like smoke, swallowing their footsteps as they bolted toward Misttvale Crossing.

But suddenly, a strangled cry escaped Jake's lips. "Someone... someone's holding my hand!" he gasped, his voice raw with panic. "I can't see him!"

Cyrus risked a glance back, and what he saw sent a jolt of horror through his body. Running alongside Jake, gripping his arm with an unnatural strength, was an old man. His skull was split open, blood pouring down his face, and one of his arms hung grotesquely at his side, clearly broken in several places. Worse still, the old man's face was twisted into a sinister grin, his teeth jagged and yellow, his dead eyes gleaming with a sickening delight.

"Jake! Get away from him!" Cyrus screamed, but Jake, too terrified to stop, kept running, his eyes wide with confusion. "What are you talking about?" he shouted. "There's no one there!"

Evelyn gasped, her face pale as she dared a glance back. "Oh God... Jake, he's right there!"

But Jake shook his head wildly, ignoring the others, his breathing ragged. "I don't see anything!" he yelled; his pace unrelenting. "We can't stop now! Just keep running!"

The ghost's bony fingers dug into Jake's arm, but still, he kept going, ignoring the tightening grip as if he were in a trance. His feet carried him faster, driven by sheer instinct. The eerie figure, smiling wickedly, continued to run alongside him, never tiring, never faltering.

Finally, they burst out of the thicket and into open air, gasping for breath. The oppressive fog began to thin, but the shadow of Misttvale Crossing loomed before them. The old man let go of Jake's hand just as they reached the edge of the forest. With one last blood-chilling smile, he faded into the mist like smoke dissolving into the night.

"What... was that?" Evelyn gasped, clutching her chest, her eyes wide with fear. Jake, pale and trembling, shook his head, still too stunned to respond.

"He was right next to you, Jake," Cyrus panted, still shaken by the sight. "Running with us. Didn't you feel it?"

Jake rubbed his arm, confusion clouding his face. "I... I don't know what you're talking about. I felt something, but I didn't see anyone. I just—" He stopped short, looking down at his arm. Dark, bloody fingerprints circled his wrist where the ghost had grabbed him.

Cyrus's stomach twisted. "We have to move," he said, his voice steely. "We can't let whatever that thing was follow us here."

The trio turned to face Misttvale Crossing.

CHAPTER THREE

Misttvale Crossing - The Real Mystery Begins

The bridge stretched out before them, a relic of another time. Cracked stones lined the path, some crumbling into the dark waters below, which seemed unnaturally still. The air here was colder, more oppressive, as if the crossing held its own secrets, its own curse. The stories surrounding this place weren't just village tales—they were warnings.

Cyrus could feel it. The shadows in the thicket had been terrifying, but here, at the Crossing, there was something far worse lurking. The weight of years of fear and loss hung in the air like a noose tightening around them.

"I hate this place," Jake muttered, his voice barely audible. "Why did Victor want us to come here?"

"Because this place holds the truth," Evelyn said softly, her eyes scanning the stone path ahead. "Victor was part of the group that vanished here all those years ago. Maybe... maybe they're all still here. Stuck."

"Stuck?" Cyrus's voice was a low growl. "What do you mean 'stuck'? You think this bridge is some kind of... prison?"

Evelyn nodded slowly. "I don't know for sure, but there's something about this place. Like it's a boundary between our world and... theirs." She gestured toward the swirling mist over the water, which seemed to ripple as if something beneath the surface was moving, waiting.

As they cautiously stepped onto the bridge, a sudden gust of wind blew from the far side, carrying with it a bone-chilling moan. The fog thickened again, coiling around them like tendrils. Shadows began to flicker at the edges of their vision—more figures, indistinct but watching.

"What now?" Jake asked, his voice wavering. He looked to Cyrus for direction, but Cyrus, too, was unsure. They were deep in it now, surrounded by forces they didn't understand.

Suddenly, Evelyn stopped, her eyes wide with realization. "Look," she whispered, pointing to the far side of the bridge.

There, faint but visible through the mist, was a symbol carved into the stone—a strange, swirling mark, the same symbol Victor had shown Evelyn in her vision. It glowed faintly, pulsing with a rhythm that made the hairs on Cyrus's arms stand on end.

"We need to reach it," Evelyn said, her voice low but firm. "That symbol... it's the key."

Cyrus swallowed hard. "Let's go. But stay close. No splitting up."

As they moved cautiously toward the symbol, the shadows around them began to shift. The figures that had lingered at the edges of the mist now stepped forward, their forms flickering in and out of sight. One by one, they appeared on the bridge—dozens of them, their faces pale and hollow, their eyes empty voids. The lost souls of Misttvale Crossing.

"We're not alone," Jake whispered, his voice shaking as the spectral figures closed in around them.

"Keep going," Cyrus urged, his heart hammering in his chest. "Just keep going!"

But the spirits seemed to press in, their hollow gazes fixed on the trio as if waiting for something—waiting for a reason to strike.

"Why aren't they attacking?" Jake asked, panic creeping into his voice. "Why are they just watching us?"

"They're waiting," Evelyn said, her voice trembling. "For us to make a mistake."

Cyrus's gaze locked onto the symbol ahead, glowing brighter now, as if calling to them. "We don't stop," he said, his voice hard. "We reach that symbol, and we find out why Victor led us here."

But as they neared the mark, the spirits moved closer, their forms shifting and twisting, whispers rising in the fog. A chorus of voices filled the air, disjointed and eerie. Words began to form, fragmented and broken:

"You... cannot... leave..."

Cyrus's pulse quickened. "We're almost there. Just a little further..."

The wind howled as the figures grew bolder, their twisted faces becoming clearer, their broken forms more solid. Misttvale Crossing was alive with the lost souls of the vanished—and the trio was walking straight into their domain.

As they reached the stone, the air seemed to grow colder, and the fog around them thickened. With a mix of desperation and curiosity, Jake and Cyrus jumped toward the stone and touched its surface. The moment their fingers brushed the ancient rock, a low, guttural noise erupted around them—echoing voices, twisted in agony.

The ghostly apparitions that had been circling them, silently watching, suddenly contorted. Their hollow faces twisted into expressions of unbearable pain as they let out a chorus of chilling, blood-curdling screams. The sound pierced the air, resonating deep within the trio, sending shivers down their spines.

The Specters shrieked as though in torment, their forms flickering and writhing like smoke caught in a violent wind.

Then, as quickly as it had begun, the noise stopped. The spirits, still writhing in agony, dissolved into the mist, one by one, until the bridge was eerily silent.

Evelyn, her heart pounding in her chest, turned her gaze to the stone. In the faint light of the coming dawn, something sinister became clear. Her eyes widened in horror. "It's blood," she gasped. "It's written in blood!"

Cyrus knelt down, inspecting the surface more closely. His breath caught in his throat. "She's right," he muttered. "It's fresh... just a day or two old."

"Wait," Jake said, squinting at the inscription. "Let me read it." He leaned in, his voice wavering as he made out the dark, crimson letters. "'Have a safe trip, Finch.'"

Cyrus's face paled. "Finch? Harold Finch? The mayor?"

Evelyn's mind raced. "Does this mean... someone killed him?" Her voice trembled with the weight of the possibility.

Jake shook his head in confusion. "It can't be. The blood's fresh, but we saw Mayor Finch at the festival, alive and well. Just yesterday. How can it be?"

Cyrus narrowed his eyes, his thoughts spinning. "Whose blood is this, then? And why is his name carved here, in the middle of all this madness?"

"And why did the shadows scream when we touched the stone?" Evelyn added, a shiver running down her spine. "Why did they disappear?"

The three of them stood in silence, staring at the cryptic message. The weight of it hung heavily in the air, shrouded in mystery.

Before they could discuss further, Cyrus felt an overwhelming urge to turn back toward the path leading out of the forest. "Finnian... we left him with Grayson."

Evelyn's eyes softened with worry. "He must be terrified. We have to get back."

Suddenly, as if on cue, Finnian's voice echoed faintly through the mist. "Cyrus!" It was distant but unmistakable.

Without a word, they all sprinted through the thinning fog, hearts pounding, until they burst through the edge of the thicket. In the clearing ahead, Finnian stood with Old Man Grayson by his side, staring at the morning light creeping over the horizon.

"Finnian!" Cyrus called, relief flooding his chest as he ran to his brother.

Finnian looked shaken but unharmed. "Cyrus... I—" He hesitated, glancing nervously toward Cyrus. "The fog... it kept whispering to me, but Grayson... he told me to stay calm, that you'd come back."

Cyrus embraced his brother briefly, guilt gnawing at him for leaving him behind. "I'm sorry, Finnian. Are you okay?"

"Yeah, I'm okay. Are you?" Finnian asked, hugging Cyrus tightly.

"I am, don't worry. But look, we found something strange." Cyrus gestured toward the stone.

Finnian glanced down at the blood-streaked surface, his eyes widening in shock. "What... what is this?" he muttered, then added with a note of alarm, "I saw the mayor just before I came here. He was walking out of the thicket, smiling... but there was something off about it. Like he knew something we don't."

Evelyn's eyes narrowed. "Something's definitely not right. We need to figure out what's going on."

As the first light of dawn broke over the horizon, casting an eerie glow over the misty forest, the four exchanged uneasy glances.

"It's time to head back to Ebonvale," Cyrus said firmly. "We need to find Mayor Finch and get some answers."

With that, they set off, the weight of the mystery pressing heavier with each step, the quiet morning air unable to chase away the lingering shadows in their minds.

CHAPTER FOUR

Echoes Beneath the Lanterns

As the group entered Ebonvale, the village was bathed in the soft morning light. The early risers were already setting up for the final day of the Lantern Festival, but the air seemed heavier than before, as though the forest's ominous presence had followed them back. The narrow streets were lined with thatched-roof cottages, their worn exteriors and creaking doors giving the village an aged and forgotten look.

The four of them stopped just outside the town square. In the distance, Mayor Harold Finch could be seen talking to a group of villagers near the festival stage, his back to them. He was a stout man, with graying hair slicked back and a constant, almost unnatural, smile that stretched too wide across his face. Dressed in his usual brown vest and crisp white shirt, Finch looked every bit the picture of a respectable village leader, but his reputation had always been clouded in whispers. Some said he was far too eager to cover up the darker happenings of Ebonvale, while others thought his rise to power was more than just a matter of local politics.

Cyrus watched him closely, remembering the strange words they had read by the stone. "Have a safe trip, Finch." The thought sent a shiver down his spine. There was something undeniably wrong about the man.

"We need to talk to him," Evelyn said in a low voice. "Whatever is going on, he has to know something."

They approached the mayor cautiously, weaving through the morning bustle. Finch noticed them out of the corner of his eye and turned toward them, his smile never fading. His eyes, however, were cold and calculating.

"Ah, Cyrus, Finnian, Evelyn, Jake," Finch greeted them warmly, his tone almost too smooth. "You all look like you've seen a ghost. What brings you here so early?"

Cyrus's throat tightened, but before he could respond, Finnian blurted out, "We saw you in the thicket last night, Mayor. Right before dawn. What were you doing out there?"

The mayor's smile twitched, but he recovered quickly. "The thicket? Ah, just enjoying a late stroll. I like to clear my mind before the chaos of the festival, you know? It's easy to lose yourself in the beauty of nature."

Jake narrowed his eyes. "And the stone near Misttvale Crossing? The one covered in fresh blood with your name on it?"

Finch's smile faltered, only for a second. His eyes darkened, but his voice remained steady. "I'm afraid I don't know what you're talking about. Blood? Stones? Sounds like the festival fever is getting to your heads. I suggest you all get some rest."

Before they could press him further, a village courier hurried over to Cyrus, handing him a sealed letter with a wax crest unfamiliar to him.

“For you,” the courier said, slightly out of breath. “It was delivered just this morning.”

Cyrus took the letter, his hands suddenly cold. He broke the seal and unfolded the note, the handwriting jagged and frantic:

"The shadows know. The blood is only the beginning. Turn back now or watch your brother disappear like the others. We are always watching, Cyrus."

His heart pounded in his chest as he read the last line:

"You don't have long. Signed, A Friend in the Fog."

Cyrus's hands trembled as he looked up at the others. "We're being watched," he whispered, his voice tight with fear.

Evelyn grabbed the letter from his hands, scanning the words quickly. "What does this mean? Who's 'A Friend in the Fog'?"

Finnian's face paled, and he took a step back, glancing nervously toward the mist that still hung low on the horizon. "Cyrus... what are we going to do?"

Before anyone could answer, Finch's smile returned—this time wider and more unsettling. "Is there a problem, boys?"

Cyrus tucked the letter into his pocket. "Nothing we can't handle, Mayor."

But as Finch turned away, a creeping dread settled over the group. Whatever was coming next, they knew it would be far worse than anything they had already faced.

Tension hung thick in the air as the group made their way toward Grayson's house. The once vibrant streets of Ebonvale now felt like a maze of shadows, each corner holding a secret waiting to be uncovered. The sun had fully risen, but its warmth did little to dispel the chill of the night's horrors still clinging to them.

As they passed the village square, the sound of hooves clattering against cobblestones drew their attention. A polished black carriage came into view, pulled by two sleek horses. The man guiding them, tall and composed, had a refined air about him, his posture immaculate even as he held the reins.

Behind him sat a figure they all recognized: Orion Wellesley.

"Cyrus, Finnian, Evelyn, Jake!" Orion's deep, calm voice cut through the stillness like a soothing balm. The man's kind eyes lit up as he waved them over, his silver hair catching the early morning light. "You all look troubled. Has something happened?"

The group paused, exchanging nervous glances. Orion Wellesley was the most generous man in Ebonvale, always helping those in need. His presence was like a beacon of hope in a village wrapped in shadows.

Cyrus gave a forced smile. "Orion... It's been a long time."

"Indeed," Orion replied, stepping down from his carriage with a gentle grace. His assistant, Anklov Welles, a broad-shouldered man with sharp eyes and a quiet demeanor, followed close behind. "It's not every day I see a group of young folks looking quite so lost in thought. What's troubling you? If there's anything I can do to help, you know where to find me. Ebonvale is my home too."

Evelyn exhaled with visible relief, as though the simple presence of Orion was enough to soothe some of the tension. "Orion, we—" She paused, glancing nervously at the others. "We've been dealing with some... strange occurrences."

Orion's eyes twinkled with curiosity, though there was a subtle sharpness in his gaze. "Strange occurrences, you say? Ebonvale is no stranger to the unusual, especially near Misttvale Crossing."

Jake stepped forward. "You've lived here for ages, Orion. You must've heard the stories."

Orion exchanged a quick look with his assistant before nodding gravely. "I have indeed. And, if you'd like, I can offer what help I can. Though I must admit, this village has more secrets than even I care to know."

Cyrus looked sceptical but intrigued. "Why would you help us?"

Orion's smile softened. "Because I believe in this town, and I want to see it thrive again. Besides, you all seem to have stirred up something... significant."

Orion's smile softened. "Because I believe in this town, and I want to see it thrive again. Besides, you all seem to have stirred up something... significant."

Cyrus nodded, though his mind churned with unease. Orion's support was appreciated, but something about the way he phrased it left Cyrus feeling like they were only scratching the surface of what was truly happening in Ebonvale. Orion's gentle nature seemed almost too well-timed, as if he was trying to steer them toward something unseen.

"We'll keep that in mind," Cyrus finally said, offering a thin smile.

With that, Orion gave a respectful nod, his assistant Anklov following behind, and they watched the two fade into the mist of the village. The conversation with Orion left the group feeling a strange blend of reassurance and wariness, but they had no time to dwell on it.

As they walked, their conversation drifted from one unsettling event to another. The eerie whispers, the screaming shadows, the blood-written message. Each mention of it deepened the knot of anxiety in their stomachs.

Suddenly, Finnian's expression shifted, his brow furrowing as if something had tugged at the edges of his memory. "Wait... I think I saw something last night," he said, his voice low, as if reluctant to share it.

Evelyn glanced at him; curiosity piqued. "What do you mean, Finn? What did you see?"

Finnian hesitated; the details still fuzzy in his mind. "It was on the way to Misttvale Crossing... a strange symbol carved into a tree. And there was something else—coal, scattered near the base of the tree. I didn't think much of it then, but now... I don't know. It just seemed... wrong."

Cyrus's eyes narrowed. "A symbol? What did it look like?"

Finnian shook his head. "It was dark. I couldn't see it clearly, but it didn't feel like something that belonged there."

Before they could dive further into the mystery, Jake waved toward the small house ahead. "Look, there's Grayson."

The old man sat in his usual spot outside his weathered cottage, his eyes half-lidded as he puffed lazily on a cigar. The scent of tobacco mingled with the crisp morning air, a strange comfort in the midst of everything. Grayson stared at the wide blue sky, lost in his thoughts, until he noticed the group approaching.

"Well, well," Grayson greeted, leaning forward slightly. "If it isn't my favourite troublemakers. You all look like you've been through hell." His gravelly voice carried a hint of amusement, but his keen eyes missed nothing. “Everything okay?”

"Not exactly," Jake replied, trying to sound casual as they all moved closer. "We... ran into a few things last night."

"Few things?" Grayson exhaled a plume of smoke, a curious eyebrow rising. "Sounds like more than a few."

They exchanged glances, and then Cyrus stepped forward, explaining everything—about the shadows at Misttvale Crossing, the stone with the blood-written message, and the cryptic letter they’d just received.

Grayson listened in silence, the amusement draining from his face the further Cyrus went. His gaze grew sharper, more focused, especially when Finnian mentioned the strange symbol and the coal.

"So... what do you make of all this?" Cyrus asked once they’d finished, his voice betraying a hint of desperation.

Grayson took another long drag of his cigar before speaking, his tone now serious. "You lot have stirred up something much bigger than you realize." He paused, tapping the ash from his cigar. "That letter, the stone, the shadows... they’re all connected. And none of it is good. If the Mayor’s name is involved, then things are darker than even I thought."

Evelyn stepped forward; anxiety evident in her voice. "What should we do, Grayson? This is beyond us. How do we stop it?"

Grayson gave her a long, thoughtful look. "Stop it? You can’t just stop something like this. The blood, the screams you heard—those aren’t things you fix with a simple answer." His eyes flicked to Finnian. "That symbol you saw... and the coal. That might be the key to understanding what’s really going on."

Finnian frowned. "But what does it mean? Is it some sort of warning?"

Grayson sighed deeply. "A symbol like that... carved in the thicket, near coal? Could be an old ritual mark, something to bind or summon spirits. The coal suggests it was part of a fire—could mean someone’s trying to wake something up, or worse, keep something hidden."

"Keep something hidden?" Jake echoed, a chill running down his spine. "You mean like... a secret?"

"Or a curse," Grayson added grimly. "Ebonvale's got plenty of those. It's an old place, full of ghosts and sins that never quite stay buried. The mayor's been too eager to brush everything under the rug, but you can't hide from the past forever."

Evelyn shuddered, crossing her arms. "So, what do we do now? Wait for the next nightmare to find us?"

Grayson leaned back, considering his next words carefully. "If you want answers, you'll have to dig deeper. That stone, that letter—it's all leading you somewhere. If I were you, I'd start with that symbol Finnian saw. Whoever carved it knew what they were doing. And the mayor... he's more involved in this than he's letting on."

Cyrus nodded, determination hardening in his expression. "Then we'll head back to the thicket. Find that symbol, see if it leads us to anything."

Grayson gave a solemn nod, his eyes shadowed with the weight of what they were about to uncover. "Be careful, kids. Ebonvale's ghosts don't like to be disturbed. And if you go looking, you might find more than you bargained for."

CHAPTER FIVE

VEIL OF DREAD

The group is now torn between two leads: the mysterious symbol in the thicket that Finnian saw and Mayor Finch's suspicious behaviour. While the letter's warning looms over them, the sense of time running out adds urgency. As they prepare to head back to the thicket to investigate the symbol, strange things start happening in the village—people acting unusual, whispers about disappearances during previous Lantern Festivals, and more ghostly appearances.

The mystery deepens, especially regarding what role Mayor Finch truly plays. The symbol, the stone, and the shadows are all part of an older, darker history of Ebonvale that has been long forgotten... until now.

After their tense conversation with Grayson, the group huddled close, feeling the weight of the mystery pressing down on them. It was clear now that the situation was much larger and more sinister than they'd first realized. The biggest question hung heavily in the air: why was Mayor Finch's name written on that stone in blood? What connection did he have to the shadows?

Their minds swirled with unanswered questions as they discussed their next steps, trying to make sense of everything. That's when Jake, scanning the horizon, suddenly froze. He stood up on a large stone for a better view, his eyes widening.

“Smoke,” Jake said, his voice sharp with alarm. “It’s coming from the village center. I think there’s a fire!”

The others snapped to attention, panic setting in. Without a second thought, they bolted from Grayson’s yard and sprinted toward the heart of Ebonvale. As they neared the village square, the sight that greeted them wasn’t what they expected.

There was fire, yes, and thick plumes of black smoke rising into the air, but something about it felt... wrong.

The fire didn’t roar with the intensity they expected—it was eerily controlled, like it was marking something specific.

"Stay back!" a familiar voice called. Orion Wellesley, appearing through the smoke, gestured for them to keep their distance. His calm demeanor seemed almost unnatural in the midst of the chaos. "This isn’t just any fire. It’s deliberate, but we’ll manage it." He quickly directed them to a safer spot.

His assistant, Anklov Welles, was frantically working to put out the flames, his face streaked with soot and sweat. "Keep away from the blaze!" hc shouted, spraying water with fierce determination. But as he worked, his voice dropped, muttering darkly. "This... this is what happens when people dig too deep. Secrets buried for a reason. If anyone continues, Ebonvale will burn in more ways than one."

Evelyn’s eyes widened at the ominous warning, but she bit her lip, saying nothing. Orion, hearing Anklov’s muttering, shot his assistant a look but didn’t contradict him.

“We need to handle this quickly,” Orion said, turning back to the group, “but once the fire’s out, we’ll have to talk. There are things... coming to light.” His eyes, as always, held a kindness, but something in his tone suggested he was just as aware of the deeper mysteries lurking beneath Ebonvale as the group was.

As Anklov worked to smother the remaining flames, the fire seemed to lose its hold, and the group stood silently watching the embers die. But even as the flames diminished, the fear Anklov’s words ignited burned brighter in their minds.

Cyrus glanced at the others, his resolve firming. Whatever was happening in Ebonvale, they were now too deep to turn back.Top of Form

Bottom of Form

"It was not spreading," Evelyn said breathlessly, her voice full of confusion as she slowed her pace.

Cyrus nodded grimly. "It's like it was burning in one spot but not moving."

There was no wind, no heat coming off the blaze, no signs of panic—just an eerie stillness that sent chills down their spines.

Finnian was the first to speak. "This... isn't right. Something was wrong with that fire. It didn't feel real."

Cyrus narrowed his eyes. "You're right. It was like a signal, a distraction." He glanced around, his instincts on edge. "Whatever that was... it was not just fire. It was something else."

In moments, the fire was gone, leaving no trace behind—not even ash. Only the lingering smell of smoke remained in the air.

Evelyn took a step back, her pulse quickening. "What just happened? That's not normal. There's something we're missing."

Before anyone could respond, the eerie silence of the square was shattered by the distant chime of the village clock. The day had passed without them noticing, and as the sun dipped below the horizon, the familiar fog began to roll in, cloaking Ebonvale once again.

Later that night...

Cyrus sat by the window of his small home, staring out at the village streets, lost in thought. The earlier fire—or whatever it had been—kept replaying in his mind. Nothing in Ebonvale was making sense anymore. The shadows, the stone, the cryptic message about Mayor Finch—it was all becoming too much.

Suddenly, a soft knock echoed from the front door, snapping him out of his thoughts. He frowned, getting up slowly, unsure if he had imagined the sound. When the knock came again, more urgent this time, Cyrus cautiously approached the door and pulled it open.

No one was there.

His heart skipped a beat as he stepped outside, scanning the street. There was no sign of anyone, but something caught his eye. A figure—distant but unmistakable—was moving swiftly toward the edge of the village, heading in the direction of the thicket.

"Cyrus?" Evelyn's voice called from inside, startled by the open door. "Who was it?"

Cyrus didn't answer immediately, his eyes fixed on the retreating figure. "I don't know... but we need to follow."

The group gathered quickly, and without wasting any time, they followed the shadowy figure into the thicket. The night air was cold and still, the fog wrapping around them like an invisible hand, pulling them deeper into the dark. As they reached the clearing near Misttvale Crossing, the figure they had been chasing disappeared into the mist.

But something else caught their attention. The stone they had encountered earlier now stood eerily illuminated by the pale moonlight, and the strange, blood-carved message remained, fresh as ever.

"We're back here..." Finnian said, his voice low and uneasy. "Why?"

Before anyone could respond, the ground beneath them began to tremble. The stone shifted slightly, as if something beneath it had stirred. A deep, rumbling sound emerged from below, echoing across the crossing like a distant scream.

Jake took a step back, eyes wide. "What the hell is happening?"

Cyrus moved closer to the stone, his breath quickening. "It's the stone... it's connected to something underneath."

Without warning, the stone cracked open, revealing a hidden passage leading down into the earth. The air that wafted up from below was cold and thick, carrying with it the unmistakable scent of decay.

Evelyn shuddered. "Do we... go down there?"

Cyrus, his face set with grim determination, nodded. “We have to. This is part of the answer. Whatever’s down there... it’s tied to the shadows. To Mayor Finch. And to this place.”

The group exchanged uneasy glances before descending into the dark passage, their lanterns flickering faintly as they went deeper. The tunnel walls were lined with old carvings, symbols similar to the one Finnian had seen on the tree earlier.

At the end of the tunnel, they came upon a small underground chamber. In the center was a stone altar, covered in the same strange symbols, and behind it stood a weathered sign—partially broken—that read, “Echoing Hollow.”

Evelyn’s voice broke the heavy silence. “The Echoing Hollow... I’ve heard the name before. It’s supposed to be haunted... but no one’s ever found it.”

Finnian nodded slowly. “We just did. And whatever’s here... it’s worse than we thought.”

Suddenly, from the darkness, a soft, ghostly whisper echoed around them, sending chills through their bones. "You’re not supposed to be here..."

The mystery of Misttvale Crossing had led them to the Echoing Hollow, the haunted valley but it was clear now that they had only scratched the surface of a much older, far darker secret.

CHAPTER SIX

Echoing Hollow: The New Mystery

Echoing Hollow, the name itself was enough to strike fear into anyone in Ebonvale. It was a place few dared to speak of openly, a valley long forgotten by most, except in whispered tales about spirits and curses.

The villagers claimed it was cursed because of events that happened many generations ago. Some said that a tragedy befell the valley—an entire family vanished one night without a trace, and their voices had been heard echoing through the mist ever since, calling for help. Others believed it was a place where forbidden rituals were held, where ancient evils were awakened. Those who ventured too close were never seen again, or if they returned, they were changed—driven mad by what they encountered there.

As the group descended deeper into the passage, the air grew colder, and the soft flickering of their lanterns cast long, unsettling shadows along the walls. The stone carvings they passed depicted strange symbols—like the one Finnian had seen on the tree earlier—symbols that seemed to pulse with an eerie life of their own, as though watching them.

A haunting wind swept through the tunnel, carrying with it a whisper—soft and indistinct, like voices carried from another world. *You shouldn't be here...*

Evelyn froze, her face going pale. "Did you hear that?"

Cyrus, keeping his voice steady, nodded. "We're not alone down here."

The group pressed on, the weight of the unknown bearing down on them. When they finally reached the underground chamber, the air felt thick with tension, as though the very walls were alive with secrets. The altar in the center drew their attention, but it was the weathered sign behind it that sent a shiver through all of them: *Echoing Hollow.*

Jake broke the silence, his voice shaking slightly. "This is it... the valley."

Evelyn nodded, swallowing hard. "But... why was it hidden beneath Misttvale Crossing? And why did the shadows scream when we touched the stone?"

Finnian knelt beside the altar, his fingers tracing the strange markings. "These symbols... they're ancient, older than anything we've seen in Ebonvale."

Before they could ponder further, a sudden movement from the shadows caught their attention. A figure stepped out from the darkness—an old man, his face obscured by a hood. His presence was ghostly, but there was something too solid, too real, about him.

"You've come too far," he rasped. His voice was barely a whisper, but it echoed through the chamber, sending chills down their spines.

Cyrus stepped forward. "Who are you? And what's going on here?"

The figure smiled, but it was a cruel, twisted smile. "The secrets of Echoing Hollow are not for you to uncover... but now that you've come this far, there's no turning back."

Suddenly, from behind them, more whispers echoed through the chamber. Dark shapes moved in the periphery of their vision, shadows that flickered and danced with an unnatural life. But these were not the same ghosts they had encountered before—these shadows moved with purpose, with intelligence.

Evelyn gasped. "Those shadows... they're not all ghosts."

Cyrus's eyes widened in realization. "Some of them are real people... pretending to be spirits. They've been hiding something."

The figure let out a low, menacing laugh. "Clever, but it won't save you."

In that moment, the mystery of Misttvale Crossing had been unraveled—there were two kinds of shadows in Ebonvale: the restless dead and those who masqueraded as them to keep prying eyes away from the truth. And that truth, whatever it was, lay deep within Echoing Hollow.

But before they could confront the old man, the chamber suddenly shook violently. Stones fell from the ceiling, and the ground trembled beneath their feet. The old man's form began to flicker and dissolve, merging with the shadows around him.

"You've unleashed something far worse than you realize," his voice echoed ominously. "The valley will consume you all."

And with that, the figure vanished.

The group stood in stunned silence, their hearts pounding. They had solved one mystery, but in doing so, they had opened the door to something far darker.

Evelyn's voice trembled as she spoke. "What now?"

Cyrus, his face set with determination, glanced back toward the passage. "We go to Echoing Hollow... we finish this."

After unravelling the eerie enigma of Misttvale Crossing, the group learned the unsettling truth: the shadows that haunted the area were not restless spirits, but living men, using the darkness and fear to conceal a more sinister plan. The next chapter awaited them in the haunted valley—Echoing Hollow, where the true secrets of Ebonvale and Mayor Finch's sinister connection to the shadows would finally be revealed. But they knew now, more than ever, that whatever they faced in the valley would test not only their courage but their very sanity.

CHAPTER SEVEN

Echoing Hollow: Beyond Misttvale Crossing

"Cyrus, look here!" Finnian's voice broke through the tense silence. He pointed toward the ground. "There are pieces of coal. Remember what I told you? I saw some near the tree in the thicket. And now... look, more here."

Cyrus crouched, inspecting the coal pieces closely. His brow furrowed. "Coal? In Ebonvale?" He stood, glancing at the others. "That's strange. We've always traded for fuel from other towns, but coal... it's never been here. There's something going on, and we're not seeing the full picture."

Jake folded his arms, eyes shifting between the stones and the coals. "So, we've got fake shadows, mysterious coal, and some cryptic message written in blood about the mayor. This keeps getting weirder."

Evelyn sighed, pushing back a stray lock of hair. "Great, now we just need an actual ghost to top it all off. Should we start digging or... wait for the ghostly tour guide?"

Jake grinned despite the tension. "Maybe if we ask nicely, the ghosts will lend us a shovel."

They shared a nervous laugh, easing the tension just enough to keep moving forward. But their laughter was short-lived as they stared at the pile of fallen stones blocking the path ahead.

"We're stuck," Finnian muttered. "How do we get out of this now?"

Cyrus sighed. "We'll find a way. There has to be one—"

Before he could finish, Evelyn leaned against the side of the chamber, wiping sweat from her forehead. Her hand pressed against a section of the wall, and with a soft *click*, the stone in front of them groaned, revealing a hidden door.

Jake's jaw dropped. "Well, I guess that counts as asking nicely!"

Evelyn blinked, startled. "Did I... did I just do that?"

Finnian chuckled, patting her on the back. "You've got the magic touch, Ev!"

Despite the brief moment of levity, the group's curiosity quickly turned back to the mystery. The new doorway beckoned ominously, leading deeper into the unknown.

Cyrus narrowed his eyes. "I don't like this, but we don't have much of a choice. We go in."

As they prepared to step into the shadowy passage, a chill ran down their spines. They couldn't help but wonder: what secrets did the Echoing Hollow hold, and what dangers awaited them inside?

The valley earned its haunted reputation due to real spirits—the ones who were wronged and now seek revenge—and living men who manipulate the fear of the dead for their own dark purposes.

The real horror begins as they realize they're not just uncovering history but triggering something dangerous.

As the group made their way deeper into the tunnel, the air grew colder, the whispering more distinct. It was as if the walls themselves were murmuring dark secrets. Their single lantern flickered weakly, casting long, trembling shadows on the damp stone walls. Cyrus led the way, gripping the lantern tightly.

Finnian followed behind him, then Evelyn, and finally Jake, who nervously brought up the rear.

The eerie silence was only broken by their hushed discussions of what they might be facing in Echoing Hollow.

Suddenly, Jake's heart raced as a cold, clammy sensation crept into his hand—the unmistakable feeling of fingers curling around his wrist. His pulse pounded in his ears, and his throat tightened with fear. He had been holding Evelyn's hand, but now... something—or someone—was gripping his other hand.

Barely able to control his voice, Jake leaned toward Evelyn, whispering with a calm he didn't feel, "Ev, listen closely. Whatever I tell you, don't react or make a sound. Just pass it on to Finnian, and tell him to pass it to Cyrus." He swallowed hard. "The thing is... someone's holding my hand from behind."

Evelyn froze, her breath catching in her throat. The hairs on the back of her neck stood up, but she forced herself not to turn around. Shaking, she nodded and whispered the message to Finnian, who instantly paled but did the same, passing the message to Cyrus.

Without a word, Cyrus raised the lantern and swung it toward the back of the line, the weak light cutting through the thick shadows that clung to them like fog.

There, behind Jake, stood a man—a ghostly figure in a faded, tattered grey dress. His skin was pale as death, his eyes hollow and dark. His face was gaunt, and his lips were drawn into a twisted, eerie smile. Blood-streaked, wild hair framed his skeletal face. His hand—a withered, bony thing—was gripping Jake's wrist tightly, though Jake could feel his cold fingers like a dead weight.

Cyrus' breath hitched, and Evelyn stifled a scream. The ghost's head twitched unnaturally, his neck cracking as he tilted it, staring straight into Jake's terrified eyes. Slowly, he opened his mouth, but no words came out—only a soft, rasping breath, like wind escaping from the grave.

“Run,” Cyrus managed to whisper, his voice trembling. But none of them moved.

Suddenly, the ghost-man let out a piercing scream, a sound that echoed through the tunnel and sent shivers down their spines. Jake yanked his hand free and stumbled forward, the group bursting into a sprint down the narrow passage, their footsteps echoing loudly in the oppressive silence. Behind them, the ghost’s chilling wail continued, his presence now felt everywhere.

They ran until they could no longer hear the screaming. Panting and gasping for breath, they finally stopped, leaning against the cold stone walls. Their faces were pale, and the atmosphere had grown even more suffocating.

Finnian, his voice shaky, looked at Cyrus. "What... what the hell was that?"

Cyrus, his face grim, shook his head. "I don’t know... but he was trying to lead us somewhere, I think."

Evelyn shuddered. "He wasn’t just any spirit. That was one of the real ones. A ghost... not someone pretending."

"Yeah, I felt that much." Jake managed a weak smile, though his hand still trembled. "He held on like he didn’t want to let me go."

Just as they began to catch their breath, they noticed something at the far end of the tunnel. Faint light was spilling through a crack in the wall, and the air felt colder, sharper, almost malevolent. They cautiously approached and found an opening leading into a vast underground chamber.

Inside, the floor was covered in strange symbols—much like the one Finnian had seen near the thicket. At the center of the chamber was an altar made of stone, with several dark objects placed upon it. The air was thick with the smell of decay, and shadows seemed to dance along the walls, though there was no light to cast them.

On the far side of the chamber stood a large, weathered sign. Though faded and broken in places, they could make out the words: “Echoing Hollow”.

Cyrus' face tightened. “This is it. The valley... we’ve found it.”

Evelyn stared at the altar in horror. “People say it’s haunted because... this is where they did it. This is where they—”

Before she could finish, the sound of footsteps echoed from the tunnel behind them, followed by that same eerie whisper: “You shouldn’t be here...”

Cyrus grabbed the lantern and pointed it toward the tunnel. But there was nothing.

Jake clenched his fists. "What do we do now? What is this place?"

“We uncover the truth,” Cyrus said, his voice filled with grim resolve. “Whatever happened in Echoing Hollow, it ties back to the village, to the mayor... and to us. But we need to be ready, because those shadows... the real ones and the ones pretending... they won’t stop.”

Evelyn glanced nervously at the altar. “We need to figure out what this place was used for. And why the spirits—”

A loud crack echoed through the chamber as the ground beneath them shook violently. Dust and debris fell from the ceiling, and the shadows seemed to twist and grow, as if they were becoming more real, more solid.

The haunting had only just begun.

CHAPTER EIGHT

Echoing Hollow: The Forgotten Dead

Finnian took a hesitant step forward, his foot landing on something hard beneath the loose earth. The sound of bones crunching under his boot sent a shiver up his spine. "What's this?" he muttered, bending down to inspect what he had stepped on.

Cyrus, sensing the urgency, brought the lantern closer, casting a faint glow across the ground. Their hearts collectively froze as they all saw it—partially buried in the dirt was an old, decayed skeleton. The bones were brittle, stained with the passage of time, and arranged in a way that made it clear the body had been there for years.

“If the ground hadn't shaken, we wouldn't have known about this,” Jake whispered, his voice unsteady. His attempt to ease the tension fell flat in the presence of the unsettling sight before them.

Nearby, a tattered leather bag lay half-buried alongside the skeleton. Cyrus crouched down, pulling the bag from the dirt. It was in terrible condition, but inside, he found an old, crumbling purse and some papers that had survived the years. Among the papers, one caught his eye—an identity card, faded and worn. The name, though barely legible, read Mark Blackwood.

"Look at this," Cyrus muttered, holding it up to the lantern's light.

Evelyn gasped, her hand covering her mouth. "Mark Blackwood? That name sounds familiar..."

Cyrus continued to rummage through the bag. Among the rotting contents, he found a document with the emblem of Ebonvale printed at the top—a tourist permit, issued years ago. The date on it was barely visible, but it indicated that Mark Blackwood had come to Ebonvale on a guided tour.

"So, he was a tourist," Evelyn murmured, her voice tinged with fear.

Finnian's eyes widened as a terrible realization dawned on him. "Maybe... maybe he was part of that group that disappeared near Misttvale Crossing. It was twenty years ago, wasn't it?"

Cyrus nodded grimly. "It fits. The tourists who were never found."

"They were murdered, then?" Jake asked, his voice strained with fear and anger.

"We don't know that yet," Cyrus replied, stuffing the papers back into the decayed bag. "But there's one person who might have answers... Mayor Harold Finch."

The weight of the discovery sank in, but their journey wasn't over. They were trapped in Echoing Hollow, and they needed a way out. As they began to search the chamber again, Evelyn stumbled upon a hidden panel in the wall, her fingers brushing against an uneven surface. She pushed against it, and with a soft creak, a secret passageway opened, revealing a narrow, winding staircase leading upward.

"This might be our way out," she whispered, her voice trembling with a mixture of hope and dread.

Cyrus nodded. "Let's move. But remember this place... we'll be back."

They hurried up the steps, emerging from a hidden entrance into the thicket, their lungs filling with fresh air after the oppressive atmosphere of the valley. They had found a way out, but Echoing Hollow's secrets still clung to them like a shadow they couldn't shake.

Back in Ebonvale, the group reconvened, the discovery of the skeleton and Mark Blackwood's identity weighing heavily on them. The suspicion surrounding Mayor Finch was growing, but confronting him directly felt too dangerous. Instead, they decided to keep an eye on him, watching from the shadows, much like the way they had been watched.

Days passed as they discreetly observed the mayor's every move. He was careful—too careful—but on the fourth night, something unexpected happened.

Late one evening, just as the village began to settle down, Finnian, who had been watching the mayor's house from a distance, saw him leave, alone and in a hurry. He signalled to the others, and together, they followed the mayor through the dark, winding streets of Ebonvale, making sure to stay hidden in the shadows.

The mayor moved swiftly, his behaviour tense, as if he was trying to avoid being seen. They followed him until he reached the old town hall, a building that had been abandoned for years.

"What's he doing here?" Jake whispered; his voice barely audible.

Cyrus held a finger to his lips, signalling for silence. They crept closer, their hearts pounding in their chests. The mayor disappeared inside the decrepit building, and after a moment of hesitation, the group quietly followed.

Inside, the air was thick with dust and the musty scent of decay. They could hear the mayor's footsteps echoing through the empty halls as he moved deeper into the building. They followed him to the basement, where a faint light flickered from behind a door.

Cyrus motioned for the others to stay back as he edged closer, peering through the crack in the door. What he saw sent a chill down his spine.

Mayor Finch was standing in front of a large, ancient-looking map of Ebonvale and its surrounding areas. On the map, one location was circled repeatedly, over and over again—the Echoing Hollow. But that wasn't all. In front of the mayor, on a small altar, was a photograph of a young man.

Cyrus' blood ran cold when he realized who the photograph was of.

It was Mark Blackwood.

The mayor reached into his coat and pulled out a knife, holding it up to the photograph, as though in some strange, twisted ritual. The group watched in horror as Finch muttered something under his breath, something dark and incomprehensible.

"What the hell is he doing?" Finnian whispered.

Evelyn's face went pale. "We need to get out of here... now."

But before they could move, the door creaked, and the mayor's head snapped toward them.

Their cover was blown.

Before Mayor Finch could spot them, a strange noise echoed from the upper floor—heavy footsteps, as though someone was dragging something across the old wood. Finch's attention snapped upward, his face contorting in confusion and suspicion. "Who's there?" he barked, his voice sharp and agitated.

No one answered. But the sound persisted, growing louder, more ominous.

The mayor, visibly unnerved, clenched his fist and began climbing the stairs, drawn by the eerie noise. Within seconds, he disappeared into one of the rooms on the second floor.

Seeing their chance, Cyrus motioned to the others to stay put. He slipped quietly out of their hiding spot and approached the large, ancient map the mayor had been studying. His eyes widened as he took in the details.

Marked across the map was a hidden route leading from Ebonvale, out into the wilderness. But what really sent a chill down his spine was the path itself—it cut straight through the Forsaken Woods, a forest long feared and avoided by the villagers, perpetually shrouded in a thick, unnatural fog. It was said that no one who ventured into the Forsaken Woods ever returned.

Even more unsettling was the fact that Misttvale Crossing had been highlighted with a bold mark, suggesting it held more significance than they had previously thought. Cyrus could feel his pulse quicken as he realized the implications—Misttvale Crossing was only the beginning. Whatever Mayor Finch was involved in, it tied back to the forest, and perhaps to the supernatural forces that haunted Ebonvale.

Before Cyrus could absorb more, he heard the mayor's voice again—this time filled with rage as he cursed the mysterious figure for distracting him. Cyrus swiftly backed away from the map and ducked into the shadows where the others were hiding.

The group exchanged silent, wide-eyed glances as they realized they were now deeper into a mystery that was far larger—and more dangerous—than they'd ever imagined.

CHAPTER NINE

Echoing Hollow: Into the Heart of Darkness

Back in the relative safety of Cyrus' house, the group gathered around the table, their expressions darkened by what they had learned. They now had two mysteries to untangle—what was Mayor Finch's connection to the Forsaken Woods, and how did this route tie back to the Echoing Hollow and Misttvale Crossing?

Jake broke the tense silence. "So, we're dealing with a cursed valley, missing tourists, fake ghosts, real ghosts, and now a mayor who's sneaking around like a villain in a cheap novel."

Finnian smirked, trying to ease the tension. "You've always been one for adventure, haven't you, Jake?"

"I'd prefer if this one didn't involve possibly getting murdered by vengeful spirits," Jake replied, half-serious.

Evelyn leaned forward; her eyes thoughtful. "But why would the mayor care about the Forsaken Woods? And why go through Misttvale Crossing to get there? There has to be something he's hiding in that forest... something tied to the shadows we've seen."

"Maybe the shadows aren't just about Echoing Hollow," Finnian said. "Maybe the Forsaken Woods has something darker in it than we've imagined. We need to find out."

Cyrus nodded; his face grim. "There's only one way to figure this out. We need to go back to Echoing Hollow, but this time, we'll be better prepared. We need to get to the bottom of whatever Mayor Finch is involved in."

Later that night, as they prepared to return to the hollow, a growing sense of dread settled over them. The village was quiet, unnervingly so, as they slipped out of Cyrus' house and made their way toward the thicket. The lantern's light barely cut through the thickening mist as they retraced their steps, following the secret passage that had led them to the hidden valley.

The deeper they went, the more oppressive the atmosphere became. The whispers in the air returned, but this time they seemed louder, more insistent. Strange shapes flitted through the fog, and the distant wail of something inhuman pierced the night.

When they finally emerged back into the cursed valley of Echoing Hollow, the group felt a wave of unnatural cold wash over them. The trees here seemed to sway with a life of their own, and the very ground beneath their feet pulsed faintly, as if the valley itself was alive, aware of their presence.

Suddenly, the lantern flickered, and Cyrus halted. "Everyone... stay close," he whispered. But just as the words left his mouth, a soft, sinister laugh echoed around them—disembodied, chilling, and growing louder.

From the fog, the figure of the grey-clad woman emerged again, her face pale and gaunt, her empty eyes staring straight at them. "You shouldn't have returned," she whispered, her voice thick with malice. "This place... it doesn't forgive."

Before they could react, the ground trembled violently, and the shadows around them began to take form. Dozens of figures appeared—some clearly spectral, with hollow eyes and transparent skin, but others seemed human, masked, and cloaked in dark robes.

Jake's eyes widened in terror. "What the hell are those?"

Cyrus gritted his teeth. "Both... it's both kinds of shadows."

Evelyn's hand trembled as she held onto Finnian. "We need to find out why they're here... why they're protecting this place."

Finnian, his face set with determination, pointed to an old, crumbling structure in the distance. "That's our next stop. Whatever's in there, it's the key to understanding this."

As they moved toward the dilapidated building, the shadows seemed to follow them, whispering ominous warnings. The deeper they ventured into the valley, the closer they came to unlocking the terrible truth that lay hidden in the Echoing Hollow.

And whatever it was, it had been waiting for them.

The narrow entrance loomed before them like the mouth of a beast, waiting to swallow them whole. Cyrus led the group inside, their breath echoing in the confined space. The air grew colder with every step, thick with an unsettling energy, as if the valley itself resented their presence. They had ventured into the Echoing Hollow again—only this time, something was different.

The moment they all stepped through, a loud thud echoed from behind.

The entrance had sealed itself.

"What the hell?" Jake cursed, spinning around to see the stone door completely shut. They were trapped, locked inside the depths of the haunted valley. The dim light from the two lanterns flickered weakly, casting twisted shadows on the damp walls.

Cyrus took a deep breath, trying to calm his pounding heart. "It's do or die, guys. We have to find another way out... and fast. We're not leaving until we figure out what's really going on here." His voice was steady, but the grim determination in his eyes said it all.

The group exchanged uneasy glances but nodded in agreement.

As they pressed on, something caught Finnian's eye. "Wait," he said, pointing ahead. "There's a tunnel. We missed it last time."

The narrow opening stretched out like a gaping wound in the rock. They cautiously stepped inside, the walls damp and the air suffocating. After a few minutes of walking, they stumbled upon something alarming—fresh footprints.

"These weren't here before," Evelyn whispered, her voice barely audible over the thudding of her heart. "Someone's been here... recently."

Finnian crouched to inspect them closer. "If we follow these, maybe they'll lead us to an exit."

The group followed the footprints deeper into the tunnel, their footsteps echoing in the eerie silence. The whispers they'd heard before were now faint murmurs, growing louder and then retreating, as if teasing them.

Then, they reached a crossroads.

Three separate paths split from the tunnel, each one stretching into the unknown. But the footprints vanished—there were no more clues to follow, only rocky ground ahead.

"This feels like a trap," Jake muttered under his breath, his eyes scanning the paths with growing unease. "Whatever we choose, it could lead us straight into something worse."

Finnian, frustrated, kicked a stone down one of the tunnels. "Great. A dead end with choices."

Cyrus glanced toward the left, feeling a faint draft. "Let's try this way."

The group moved cautiously down the left path, the shadows seeming to grow darker as they progressed. They walked in silence, each of them on edge, until a faint light appeared at the end of the tunnel. As they got closer, the source of the light became clear—the old town hall of Ebonvale—known locally as Forsaken Hall.

Evelyn gasped; her voice filled with disbelief. "How did this end up here?"

The building stood like a decrepit skeleton, its structure half-decayed, the windows shattered. Inside, faint lantern light flickered from an unseen source. As they drew nearer, they realized this wasn't the first time someone had been here recently.

"This is where Finch was," Cyrus said, narrowing his eyes. "This is the same hall where the mayor was watching that map."

Finnian looked confused. "But how did the tunnel connect to this place?"

Cyrus didn't have an answer. "Let's get inside and find out."

Inside the hall, everything was quiet—too quiet. The air felt heavy with the weight of forgotten years, dust hanging in the faint light of their lanterns. They crept through the rotting building, footsteps echoing off the creaky floorboards.

It wasn't long before they found what they had come for.

There, on the central table, was the map—the same one Mayor Finch had been inspecting earlier that day. Cyrus' eyes widened in recognition as he approached it. The lantern cast a dim glow over the paper, revealing routes leading out of Ebonvale.

"It's the same map," Cyrus whispered, tracing the lines with his fingers. "He marked a route... through Forsaken Woods... and Misttvale Crossing."

Jake's face twisted in confusion. "Wait, why's he marking all this? What's he hiding?"

Evelyn looked over Cyrus' shoulder, her voice tense. "There's something circled on the map. Right in the middle of the woods."

Cyrus squinted at the faded writing. "It says, 'The Heart of Shadows.'"

CHAPTER TEN

The Forsaken Hall's Horrors

Before they could process it, a loud creak echoed from above them, the unmistakable sound of footsteps. Mayor Finch's familiar voice rang out. "Who's there?"

The group froze, eyes wide. The mayor had returned.

In a panic, they darted behind an old bookshelf, barely making it out of sight before Finch's footsteps approached. The mayor snapped his head around, clearly on edge.

"Who's there?" he barked again, his voice trembling slightly.

The sound of heavy, deliberate footsteps followed from upstairs. Someone—or something—was up there.

Mayor Finch cursed under his breath, grabbing a lantern as he hurried up the stairs to investigate the noise. This was their chance.

"Now's our time," Cyrus whispered urgently, motioning to the map. He dashed back to the table and quickly scanned it, noticing something else—the mayor had marked a hidden path leading out of the village, straight through Forsaken Woods.

But what shocked Cyrus most was the large red 'X' over Misttvale Crossing. Before he could take it all in, Finch's voice echoed down from upstairs. The group immediately slipped back into their hiding place as the mayor descended, muttering about the strange noise upstairs.

Cyrus backed off, heart pounding, just as Finch re-entered the hall. The group held their breath, waiting in the shadows, terrified they might be discovered.

As soon as Finch left the building, the group quickly regrouped, trying to piece together what they had seen.

"He's hiding something massive," Cyrus muttered, his brow furrowed. "He knows the way out—and more. He's marking places on that map for a reason."

"We need to get out of here," Evelyn said urgently. "We can't stay in this place much longer. What if he comes back?"

"There's more to this," Finnian said, his voice thoughtful. "That 'Heart of Shadows' he marked... it's important. It has to be. Whatever is out there in the Forsaken Woods, it's tied to Echoing Hollow."

"Let's focus on getting out for now," Cyrus said. "We'll come back. We have to expose this."

As they prepared to leave, Jake stepped on a loose floorboard. Beneath it, they found something they hadn't expected—another hidden passage.

"This place is full of secrets," Finnian muttered, eyeing the dark tunnel below. "Maybe this leads to an exit."

Or perhaps... deeper into the mystery.

With no other choice, they descended once again into the unknown, unaware that the horrors of Forsaken Hall had only just begun.

As they descended into the hidden dark tunnel beneath Forsaken Hall, the air grew colder, heavier, as if the walls themselves were suffocating them. The flicker of their lanterns barely illuminated the claustrophobic space. Under their feet, something crunched unnervingly. It was too dark to see, so Cyrus and Jake turned up the flames in their lanterns, casting a wider, eerie glow around the space.

What they saw made their blood run cold.

Littered across the floor were human skeletons—bones long decayed, some half-buried in layers of dust and debris. Trash bags and tattered remnants of clothing were strewn around them, looking untouched for decades. The walls seemed to close in, haunted by the silence of death.

Evelyn's eyes widened in horror, her voice trembling. "Human skeletons... but how? Why here, in this hidden place? Whose skeletons are these?"

Finnian took a few steps forward, trying to control his racing heart. "There are bags here. Let's check them. Maybe we'll find some answers."

The group crouched down, hesitant, their fingers trembling as they searched through the bags. Dust flew up into the air, and with each item they uncovered, a clearer picture formed. Old maps, IDs, wallets—all faded with age. Then Cyrus pulled out something unmistakable.

"These... are the tourists," he said, barely above a whisper. "The ones who disappeared from Misttvale Crossing twenty years ago. They never left."

Evelyn shivered; her voice tight with fear. "But why are they down here? Who could have done this?"

"There were ten in that group, right?" Jake said, turning over one of the rotting bags. "That's what the reports said. But we've only found nine skeletons. Where's the tenth?"

Finnian's gaze swept across the bones, the eerie emptiness of the dark room pressing in on them. "Where is the tenth person?"

A chilling realization dawned on Cyrus; his voice low. "We found Mark Blackwood's body in Echoing Hollow... That means there are nine here, including him. But Victor Valtor's remains are missing."

The name sent a fresh wave of unease through the group. Evelyn's hand shot to her mouth as her memory sharpened. "Victor Valtor... His ghost is the one I saw the other night, right? But he disappeared a day after the others vanished."

Cyrus stood up, his eyes scanning the room again. "That's no coincidence. If Victor was involved somehow, why is his ghost haunting us? Was he part of this? Or was he another victim?"

The group fell silent, the weight of these questions pressing down on them like the suffocating darkness that surrounded them. Suddenly, a soft noise broke the silence—a faint whisper, a movement behind them.

"Did you hear that?" Jake whispered; his voice barely audible.

Before they could react, the tunnel itself seemed to shift, a sudden cold breeze sweeping through the underground chamber as though something was coming.

The group was shaken by their discovery, but there was no time to dwell on it. They needed to leave this cursed tunnel and solve the mystery of Echoing Hollow once and for all. They scrambled to find an exit from the forsaken passage, determined to uncover the truth behind Victor Valtor and the dead tourists. Every step felt heavier, every shadow watching them with unseen eyes.

As they finally made their way out of the underground chamber, they emerged once again in Echoing Hollow, the valley echoing with the haunting whispers of its cursed past. The thick fog swirled around them, as if alive, and the shadows loomed larger than before.

But this time, they were prepared.

CHAPTER ELEVEN

ECHOING HOLLOW'S HIDDEN CURSE

The group ventured deeper into Echoing Hollow, the fog swirling ominously around them. Each step felt laden with dread, as if the valley itself held secrets too dark to unearth. They were determined, though, driven by the mounting mysteries and strange occurrences that seemed to tie everything together.

As they walked, Finnian's mind raced, pieces of the puzzle slowly clicking together. Then something clicked. He remembered a conversation with Old Man Grayson, years ago. Grayson had once mentioned something about Echoing Hollow that he had forgotten until now.

"This valley..." Finnian whispered, stopping in his tracks. "It wasn't always like this."

The others turned to him, puzzled.

"One of the villager told me this place used to be a coal mining valley before it was closed off," Finnian continued, his eyes scanning the landscape. "It was shut down years ago because of government issues—maybe safety or some other cover story. But what if that was a lie? What if the mine never fully shut down?"

Evelyn furrowed her brow, trying to connect the dots. "You think someone's still mining here?"

Cyrus rubbed his chin thoughtfully, a flash of realization passing through his gaze. "That would explain the strange things we've seen. The coal we found scattered around the thicket and other parts of Ebonvale—there's no reason for it to be there if all coal is supposed to be imported."

Jake, always the Skeptic, folded his arms. "But if there's illegal mining happening, why go through all this trouble? Why hide it with all these ghost stories?"

"To keep people away," Finnian answered darkly. "Think about it. The legends of the haunting here, the stories about Echoing Hollow and Misttvale Crossing—they're all to scare people off. No one would come looking for anything if they thought the place was cursed."

Evelyn's eyes widened. "So, the haunting could be just a cover... to hide an illegal coal operation?"

"And not just any coal," Cyrus added, his voice tense. "Think about the Blackwater Lake. The lake that's abandoned because of the stories about Echoing Hollow. What if the other part of the valley near Blackwater Lake is still being used to extract coal? That place has been off-limits for decades."

Finnian nodded, pieces falling into place. "The lake... and this part of the valley... they could be connected. This tunnel might be part of a hidden route to smuggle coal out of Echoing Hollow, without anyone noticing."

Jake's eyes widened. "That's why they blocked off that secret tunnel! They didn't want anyone stumbling on it."

"The skeletons we found..." Evelyn said, her voice trembling. "Could they have been witnesses? People who saw too much?"

"Maybe," Cyrus said grimly. "Maybe they got too close to the truth."

A heavy silence fell over the group as the full weight of their discovery sank in. The haunting, the eerie shadows, the disappearances—it had all been part of a twisted scheme to cover up illegal mining beneath Echoing Hollow.

But before they could process any further, the distant echo of footsteps in the tunnel sent a shiver through them. Someone else was nearby.

"We're not alone," Cyrus whispered, pulling everyone closer. "We need to get out of here. Now."

With their minds reeling from the discovery of the hidden coal operation, the group hurried through the dark passages of Echoing Hollow. They needed to find the exit—and fast. The realization that they had stumbled onto something much bigger than a haunting made every shadow seem more menacing.

As they scrambled through the twisting paths, Finnian's heart raced. "If the coal is being smuggled from here to the outside, we need to figure out where the other end of this tunnel leads."

"It's got to be somewhere near the Forsaken Woods," Cyrus guessed, as the tunnel started sloping upward. "That forest has always been covered in fog, just like this valley. I bet it's where they're transferring the coal out, using the fog as cover."

Evelyn glanced back nervously, the sound of distant footsteps making her skin crawl. "What if they're onto us?"

"They probably already are," Jake muttered. "Which means we've got to stay ahead of them."

Finally, they reached an opening in the tunnel, the faint light of day breaking through the fog ahead of them. As they stepped out, they found themselves at the edge of the Forsaken Woods, the dark, looming trees stretching out in front of them. The oppressive fog thickened around them, swirling like a living thing.

"This is it," Finnian said, pointing ahead. "The other side of the smuggling route."

But as they stood there, looking out into the woods, a strange sensation washed over them. The trees seemed to whisper, the fog growing denser, darker. Something wasn't right.

"I don't like this," Evelyn said, clutching her lantern tighter. "There's something else here. Something worse than we thought."

Cyrus's face was pale, his voice steady but grim. "We've uncovered the truth about Echoing Hollow... but Forsaken Woods is another story. And whatever's hidden there, we need to be prepared."

Little did they know, they were about to confront something far more terrifying than illegal mining.

Forsaken Woods held secrets of its own.

CHAPTER TWELVE

Shadows of the Forsaken Woods

As the group entered the Forsaken Woods, the eerie atmosphere settled over them like a shroud. The trees loomed tall and twisted, their branches reaching out like skeletal hands, casting long shadows in the pale moonlight. The wind howled through the forest, carrying with it a chill that made the hair on the back of their necks stand on end.

Suddenly, a noise broke the silence.

"Someone's coming," Cyrus whispered urgently, his voice barely audible. "Everyone, hide in those bushes."

They ducked into the thick brush, just in time to see a lone figure emerge from the dense woods. With the dim glow of their lanterns lowered, they could still make out the silhouette of the man moving quickly through the trees, his long strides purposeful and hurried.

"Anklov Welles," Finnian whispered, his eyes widening. "That's Orion's assistant. What's he doing out here in the Forsaken Woods... at this hour?"

Evelyn's face tensed with unease. "I've never trusted him. Not since the fire in the village square... he was trying to scare us then, warning us about 'consequences.' But why is he here now, and alone?"

Jake squinted through the darkness, watching Anklov's hurried steps. "He seems nervous. There's something off about him."

The group stayed low, watching as Anklov passed by, his lips curled into a strange, unsettling smile. His movements were quick, almost frantic, as if he had somewhere important to be—and it wasn't long before he disappeared into the thicker part of the woods, heading toward the abandoned section of the forest, near Blackwater Lake.

"Something's wrong," Cyrus said, his voice a tight whisper. "I think we need to follow him. He might be connected to this mining operation we've been suspecting."

"But why would Orion's assistant be involved in something like that?" Finnian asked, though a creeping suspicion was already forming in his mind.

Evelyn nodded; her voice grim. "It's starting to make sense. This forest, the fog, the lake... I think they've been using these woods as a cover to smuggle coal. And Anklov knows something—something big."

Uncovering the Depths:

The group trailed Anklov deeper into the Forsaken Woods, their footsteps light and cautious. The dense trees seemed to close in around them, and the night air grew colder as they ventured further from the village. They could hear the faint sound of water in the distance—Blackwater Lake, notorious for being haunted and abandoned.

As they followed Anklov's path, the ground began to change beneath their feet. It wasn't the soft, loamy soil of the forest floor anymore, but something harder, more industrial. They reached a clearing where the trees had been cut away, and in the moonlight, they saw it: a hidden mine entrance, old but not forgotten. Tools and machinery, rusted but recently used, were scattered around, covered by branches and dirt to keep them hidden from anyone passing by.

Anklov stood at the entrance, speaking in hushed tones to a figure in the shadows. It wasn't Orion. This person was shorter, stockier, and wore a miner's helmet.

The group strained to listen.

"It's almost ready," Anklov's voice came through the darkness. "We'll make the next move soon—this mine is still valuable, and no one's going to find out. Not even those fools who are busy chasing ghosts."

Cyrus clenched his fists. They weren't just dealing with ghosts anymore. This was bigger—much bigger.

The tension in the chamber was thick as the group watched from their hiding spot. The dim lantern light flickered in the shadows, casting eerie shapes on the damp walls. As they followed the miner through the underground tunnel, their steps were hesitant, hearts pounding in their chests.

But then, something shifted in the air, colder, more oppressive. They froze. "What is that?" Jake whispered, his voice trembling. A chill swept through them, and in the dim light, they saw them—figures, spectral and faint at first, then more solid as they approached. Ghosts.

Real ghosts.

Their pale, translucent faces were twisted in expressions of agony, their clothes tattered remnants of a time long gone. The air around them buzzed with a faint whispering, like voices long dead but refusing to fade.

Cyrus took a step back. "They're... real. Oh, God. They're real."

The ghosts moved closer, their hollow eyes locking onto the group. Evelyn clutched Finnian's arm, fear gripping her. "We have to get out of here," she whispered, her voice barely audible.

Before they could move, one of the ghosts let out a low, mournful wail. It shot through them like a dagger, freezing them in place. One by one, the ghosts began to advance, hands outstretched as if to grab them. The group stumbled back, panic setting in.

A ghost lunged at Jake, its face a mask of anger, and he barely dodged out of the way. "Run! Run!" Jake yelled, his voice breaking with fear. But no matter where they turned, the ghosts were everywhere—closing in, their wails echoing in the chamber.

Cyrus held up the lantern, the light flickering wildly. "Stay back!" he shouted, but the ghosts only hesitated for a moment before resuming their relentless approach.

As they pressed themselves against the cold stone walls, Finnian, muttered under his breath, "I wasn't even this scared when I saw that ghost near Misttvale, his voice trembling. "Not even when we found Mark Blackwood's skeleton—or all those bodies under the Town Hall." he paused, swallowing hard, the weight of his fear pressing down on him. "But this... this is different."

Suddenly, something changed. The ghosts paused, as if they had heard Finnian's words. They exchanged glances, their expressions softening, confusion replacing their fury. One of them, a woman with hollow eyes and a once-elegant gown, stepped back. The other ghosts followed suit; their movements slower, less aggressive.

"They stopped..." Cyrus whispered, bewildered.

The ghosts no longer seemed intent on attacking them. Instead, they lingered, drifting back into the shadows, their eyes still fixed on the group—but now, with a strange sense of recognition. It was as though Finnian's mention of Mark Blackwood had stirred something in them.

"What... what's happening?" Evelyn asked, her voice shaking.

"I think..." Finnian swallowed hard, "...I think they know him, Mark blackwood."

The ghosts began to move toward a tunnel deeper within the mine, almost beckoning the group to follow. The air was thick with fear and uncertainty, but now there was something else—a mystery unravelling before them.

"They're not here to kill us... at least not yet," Cyrus muttered, though his voice held no certainty.

"Maybe... they want us to see something," Finnian said.

But one question burned in all their minds—why were the ghosts here, and what secret of the forsaken woods were they guarding? And as they stepped forward, following the spectral figures deeper into the mine, the true horror of what awaited them was only beginning.

The group hesitated only briefly before following the tunnel where the shadows had vanished. The air grew colder with every step, thick and stale, making it hard to breathe. The walls seemed to close in around them as their footsteps echoed eerily, the weight of the darkness pressing on their backs. But the adrenaline surging through their veins kept them moving forward, the drive to uncover the truth pushing aside the suffocating fear.

The tunnel wound deeper into the earth, twisting like the secrets of Ebonvale itself. It felt as though they were descending into the very heart of the mystery that tied Misttvale Crossing, Echoing Hollow, and the Forsaken Hall together.

Finally, a faint glow appeared ahead, and as they neared the tunnel's exit, a sickly yellow light filtered in through the cracks. They emerged into the cold night, only to find a strange sight waiting for them—a series of old, rusted mine carts, long abandoned but somehow still haunting in their presence. The remnants of illegal mining operations, no doubt, but now something far more sinister seemed to cling to them.

Ahead, shrouded in mist and shadow, stood an old, decrepit house. It loomed in the darkness like a forgotten relic, its broken windows staring back at them like hollow eyes. Weeds had grown wild around it, but the faint flicker of a light from within suggested it was not entirely abandoned. It looked like it had been lost to time, swallowed by the Forsaken Woods.

"What the hell is this place?" Jake whispered, his breath forming small clouds in the chilly air. "The more we dig into this, the deeper we get into something we can't control."

"I don't think we should go back," Evelyn said, her voice hushed but steady. "It's too late, and going through that tunnel again... I have a feeling it's not going to be safe anymore."

"So where do we go?" Finnian asked, his eyes darting around nervously.

Cyrus's gaze was fixed on the eerie house. "That place... whoever lived here must have known something. If someone's still in there, maybe they hold the answers we need."

Without another word, they cautiously made their way to the house. The front door, half off its hinges, creaked as they pushed it open. Inside, the air was thick with dust, and the smell of decay was overwhelming. The flickering light was coming from an old, rusty lantern, barely illuminating the rotting interior.

Shadows seemed to dance in every corner, and the oppressive silence was broken only by the occasional groan of the house settling, as though it were alive, watching them.

"Let's stay here for the night," Cyrus whispered, his voice barely audible in the heavy silence. "But we need to keep watch. I don't trust this place."

They moved cautiously through the dilapidated rooms, trying to find somewhere safe to rest. As they explored, strange things began to happen.

CHAPTER THIRTEEN

The Vanishing of Finnian

The temperature in the old house plummeted, the air becoming dense and frigid as an unnatural cold spread through the room. The group stood huddled together, their breaths shallow, their bodies tense. The distant sound of something heavy dragging across the floor above them pierced the silence, sending shivers down their spines.

Evelyn's voice trembled as she whispered, "What was that?"

Cyrus tightened his grip on the lantern, its flickering light casting unsettling shadows across the decaying walls. "We need to stick together," he muttered, his tone sharp and urgent. "No one splits up. Whatever's in this house... it's not friendly."

The house seemed to awaken around them. The groaning floorboards beneath their feet creaked in unnatural rhythm, as though the building itself was alive and breathing. From above, faint footsteps echoed, pacing back and forth, back and forth, in an unsettling cadence. None of them had ventured to the second floor, but it was clear—someone, or something, was up there.

A soft tapping began at the window, a slow, rhythmic knock, as though something outside was trying to get in. Jake turned toward the sound, but when he peered into the thick darkness beyond the glass, there was nothing. The window remained black and empty, save for the reflection of his own frightened face staring back at him.

“Let’s just... keep moving,” Finnian said, his voice strained, as they cautiously made their way into the next room.

The group stayed close, their breaths shallow, hearts pounding as they crossed into what must have once been a dining room. The long table, covered in dust, looked as though it hadn’t been touched in years. Broken chairs lay scattered across the floor, and old, rotting curtains fluttered weakly in the draft.

As they walked, strange, almost imperceptible sounds filled the air—faint whispers that seemed to slither through the walls, breaths that were not their own. Evelyn’s hand tightened around Jake’s arm, her knuckles white.

Suddenly, Jake’s hand shot to his chest, a sharp pain striking him. His fingers felt numb, like ice had crept into his very bones.

“Finnian?” Jake asked, his voice thick with confusion.

But there was no reply.

“Finnian, you there?” Jake repeated, his brow furrowing as he glanced to his side.

Silence.

That’s when Jake felt it—the hand he’d been holding felt wrong. Cold, unnaturally cold, and much heavier than Finnian’s. His heart skipped a beat, panic swelling inside him as he slowly turned his head, eyes wide in disbelief.

The figure standing beside him... wasn’t Finnian.

The face staring back at him was hollow, sunken, the skin pale and stretched tightly over a skeletal frame. Its eyes—black and empty—held a twisted, malevolent grin, one that sent pure terror crashing into Jake. The hand gripping his own was icy, its flesh decayed and wet, as though it had crawled out of a grave.

Jake’s scream shattered the air.

The others spun around in alarm; their faces contorted with horror as they saw the ghastly figure holding Jake’s hand. The lantern flickered violently, and suddenly, the shadows in the room seemed to swell, growing larger, stretching, and twisting around them like dark, hungry vines.

"Jake! Let go!" Cyrus shouted; his voice strained with panic.

But the cold, lifeless hand-held firm, pulling Jake deeper into the swirling shadows. The walls of the house warped and trembled, the very structure of the building groaning as though something monstrous was awakening beneath it. The air grew impossibly cold, and an overwhelming sense of dread washed over them all.

"Where's Finnian?" Evelyn shrieked, her voice cutting through the chaos.

The realization hit them all at once—Finnian was gone. Somehow, in the midst of the growing horror, he had vanished without a trace.

But the creature standing where Finnian should have been... was something else entirely.

"Finnian!" Cyrus called out, his voice echoing through the house, but there was no answer. Only the sound of the house groaning in response, the dark presence feeding off their fear.

The creature released Jake, its twisted grin widening as it slithered backward into the darkness, disappearing into the shadows as though it had never been there. Jake staggered back, gasping for breath, his skin pale with terror.

"We have to get out of here," Evelyn cried, her voice shaking. "This place... it's not safe. It never was."

But before they could move, the house seemed to shift again, the floorboards beneath them creaking loudly. Objects began to move on their own—chairs scraped across the floor, a cupboard door slammed shut with a deafening bang, and the lantern Cyrus held flickered one last time before the flame snuffed out, plunging them into complete darkness.

The tapping at the window grew louder, more insistent. And then the footsteps above them started again, only this time, they were faster, as though something was running toward them, hunting them.

Jake fumbled for his flashlight, his hands trembling as he clicked it on. The narrow beam of light cut through the thick blackness, casting long, twisted shadows that danced across the walls.

"We need to find Finnian!" Cyrus shouted; his voice barely audible over the escalating chaos.

But where was Finnian? Had the house taken him, or had something far worse happened? The thought gnawed at them, deepening their fear. They didn't know what they were up against—but whatever it was, it was playing with them, leading them deeper into its web.

Suddenly, Jake froze.

"What's wrong?" Evelyn asked, her voice trembling.

Jake swallowed hard. "I... I think... I think someone's upstairs."

The footsteps had stopped, but the heavy dragging sound had returned, now directly above them.

Cyrus turned to the others; his expression grim. "We have to go up there."

Reluctantly, they made their way to the staircase. Each step groaned under their weight, as though the house was warning them to turn back. The darkness at the top of the stairs seemed even thicker, almost alive, pulsating with a malevolent energy.

As they reached the landing, a door creaked open on its own, revealing a long, narrow hallway lined with decaying doors. Faint whispers echoed from within the rooms, barely audible, but undeniably there.

"Finnian?" Cyrus called; his voice shaky.

No answer.

They moved cautiously down the hall, passing door after door, each one creaking slightly as they walked by. The heavy dragging sound was closer now, coming from the end of the hall.

And then, they saw it—a figure, barely visible in the shadows, standing at the far end of the hallway.

"Finnian?" Evelyn whispered, her heart racing.

But as they approached, the figure didn't move. It just stood there, silent and still, its face hidden in the darkness.

Something was terribly wrong.

CHAPTER FOURTEEN

The Grave of Shadows

The figure at the end of the hallway stood motionless, shrouded in shadows. Cyrus, despite the gnawing terror that gripped him, moved closer. His breath was shallow, the lantern trembling in his hand. As he drew nearer, the figure's form became clearer—its sunken eyes glowed faintly in the dark, and its skin clung tightly to its bones like a decayed corpse.

The figure wasn't Finnian.

It was a skeleton, dressed in torn miner's clothes, caked in dirt and dust, its hollow eyes staring into nothingness. The group froze in shock, their hearts pounding as the eerie silence pressed in on them. Evelyn let out a stifled scream, and the air seemed to grow colder, more oppressive.

Suddenly, the skeleton's head jerked toward Cyrus, its bony hand slowly rising as if pointing to something beyond them. They backed away, stumbling over each other, and without another thought, ran out of the house, their terrified breaths echoing in the night.

Once outside, they were consumed by panic, shouting Finnian's name into the empty night.

"Finnian! Finnian!" Cyrus called desperately, his voice cracking with fear and frustration. But only silence answered him, the forest swallowing his cries.

Evelyn placed a hand on Cyrus's shoulder, her own eyes wide with fear. "We'll find him, Cyrus," she whispered, though even she wasn't sure.

Jake, panting from the adrenaline, suddenly stopped and pointed toward the far end of the yard. "Guys... look." His voice was barely above a whisper.

Behind the house, half-obscured by thick fog, was a cemetery. The gravestones, old and weathered, jutted out from the earth like broken teeth. But it wasn't the decay that chilled them–it was the fresh grave in the center, its dirt still loose, as though it had only recently been dug.

Cyrus, his breath shallow, approached the grave. His heart lurched when he saw the name on the headstone:

Finnian Dusk.

"No," Cyrus muttered, dropping to his knees. His hands trembled as he touched the cold, freshly turned earth. "No! This can't be real!"

Evelyn and Jake stood frozen, their minds racing, struggling to comprehend what they were seeing. The eerie stillness of the cemetery pressed in on them, amplifying the fear that crawled through their skin.

Tears welled up in Cyrus's eyes as the reality of his brother's disappearance sank in. "He was right here... we were holding hands, and now this?!" His voice cracked with emotion, raw and desperate. "Finnian!" he screamed into the fog, but again, only the eerie quiet of the woods responded.

But then, Jake saw something half-buried in the dirt at the foot of the grave. A small piece of paper, yellowed and frayed, poked out from the soil. With trembling hands, he bent down and pulled it free. Unfolding it, he saw that it was a letter, scrawled in shaky handwriting:

"Don't try to unravel the secrets of Ebonvale. Beware the real shadows, as they know everything about you. This is the last warning otherwise......."

A chill ran down Jake's spine as he read the note aloud. The group exchanged uneasy glances, the weight of the message settling heavily on them.

"Real shadows? Otherwise...?" Evelyn whispered. "What does that mean?"

Cyrus clenched his fists, his emotions battling between grief and rage. "Whoever's behind this... they took Finnian. And we're going to get him back."

"But how?" Jake asked, his voice trembling. "We're up against something beyond us. Ghosts, shadows, these graves... what if we're next?"

Evelyn knelt beside the grave, staring at the freshly turned earth. "We have to follow the clues. This letter—it's our only lead."

Just then, the wind picked up, swirling the mist around them, and a low, guttural moan echoed from the woods. The shadows between the trees began to shift, as if something—or someone—was watching them. The ground beneath their feet felt unstable, like it could collapse at any moment, and the air was thick with a presence they couldn't see but could feel, creeping closer.

"Look," Jake said, his voice barely a whisper. He pointed toward the far end of the cemetery, where another shadowy figure stood, half-hidden by the trees. It didn't move, but its gaze—cold, lifeless—was fixed on them.

Cyrus's jaw tightened. "We need to go. Now."

As they turned to leave the cemetery, the sound of earth shifting caught their attention. The freshly dug grave, Finnian's grave, began to sink in, as though something beneath the soil was pulling it down. Then, slowly, the ghostly figure at the edge of the woods began to move toward them.

"We're not alone here," Evelyn muttered, backing away. "We need to move!"

The group stumbled through the fog, back toward the house, but the sense of dread only deepened. The cemetery, the cryptic note, the figure that seemed to follow them—everything pointed toward an unspeakable truth lurking within Ebonvale's heart. And somewhere, Finnian was out there—lost, trapped, waiting for them to uncover the secret that might be their only chance to save him.

As they reached the edge of the cemetery, where a shadow was staring towards them, Cyrus looked back, his mind reeling. "We're not giving up," he said firmly. "We'll find Finnian, no matter what it takes. And we'll uncover the truth behind this cursed place."

But none of them could shake the feeling that the cemetery wasn't done with them yet.

CHAPTER FIFTEEN

FOOTSTEPS TO THE UNKNOWN

The group stood frozen, staring at the shadowy figure at the edge of the cemetery. Its outline was unclear, cloaked in a heavy mist that seemed to cling to the air. Cyrus, heart pounding, glanced at Jake and Evelyn, and without exchanging a word, they all knew what had to be done—they had to follow it. The lantern's glow wavered in Cyrus's trembling hand as they ventured deeper into the woods behind the cemetery, the towering trees of the forest swallowing them in a haunting silence.

As they pressed forward, the oppressive atmosphere of the Forsaken Woods thickened. Shadows seemed to move in the corners of their vision, but when they turned to look, there was nothing but trees. Then, from a far distance, they saw it—dark figures standing deathly still, far ahead. The shadows stood in a tight formation, eerie and unmoving, their shapes distorted by the fog, almost as if they were guarding something.

"Do you see that?" whispered Evelyn, her voice barely audible above the oppressive silence.

Cyrus nodded, eyes narrowing. "They're... waiting for something."

Before they could take another step, the sound of Jake stumbling over a branch snapped the stillness. The crack echoed through the woods. As if on cue, the shadowy figures melted away into the mist, vanishing like they were never there.

The group exchanged nervous glances and then moved forward cautiously. And there, on the ground, they saw him.

"Finnian!" Cyrus's voice was tight with panic as he rushed to his brother's side. Finnian lay unconscious on the cold forest floor, his face pale, his clothes covered in dirt and leaves. The others hurried to his side, but no matter how much they tried to rouse him, he remained unresponsive.

Cyrus knelt down, gently shaking his brother. "Finnian, wake up. Come on!" His voice trembled with urgency.

As they tried to revive him, Evelyn noticed something—a small slip of paper near Finnian's hand, half-buried beneath the leaves. She reached for it and unfolded the crumpled note. Her eyes widened as she read the chilling message.

"Tomorrow night... Forsaken Hall..."

Cyrus snatched the note from her hands, scanning the ominous words. The Forsaken Hall—the abandoned town hall of Ebonvale. "What does this mean? And why—why would someone leave this with Finnian?"

Jake, examining the note more closely, pointed out something even more unsettling. "Look at the handwriting. It's the same as the note we found before—the one that warned us."

A cold shiver ran down Cyrus's spine. The same handwriting... the same person. Whoever had kidnapped Finnian was no ghost—they were alive, lurking somewhere in the shadows of Ebonvale. And they had made a mistake. In their haste, they had left a trail.

"Look!" Evelyn gasped, pointing to the ground beside them. Fresh footprints. They led away from where Finnian lay, deeper into the forest and curving around toward the village.

Without hesitation, they followed the trail, their hearts racing with every step. The path twisted through the thick undergrowth of the Forsaken Woods, winding deeper into the darkness before emerging at a strange, unexpected place—the back of Old Man Grayson's house.

The group came to a sudden halt, staring in disbelief. "Grayson's house?" Jake whispered. "How does this path...?"

The realization hit them all at once. The shadowy figures they had seen, the strange trail—it led back to Ebonvale, and not just anywhere, but to Grayson's backyard. A circular route, hidden in plain sight, had somehow connected the haunted woods, the cemetery, and Grayson's house, all without them realizing it. The proximity of Grayson's house to the village's edge, just behind the Haunted Thicket, now felt far more ominous.

"This doesn't make sense," Cyrus muttered, still clutching the note. "How does the trail connect here?"

"Maybe we missed something," Jake said, glancing around nervously.

The group exchanged uneasy glances, the weight of unanswered questions pressing heavily on them. Why had Finnian been left in the woods? What was the connection between the Forsaken Woods, Grayson's house, and the shadowy figures? And most importantly, who had written the note and what did they want with Finnian?

But one thing was clear—whoever was behind this wasn't done with them yet. And tomorrow night, at Forsaken Hall, they would have to face whatever darkness awaited them.

With their minds racing and the chilling note in hand, they knew they had no choice but to attend the mysterious meeting. The secrets of Ebonvale were finally beginning to unravel, but what they were about to uncover might be more than they had ever bargained for.

The night settled uneasily around Cyrus's house; the air thick with anticipation. While the group prepared themselves for what the next evening would bring, the atmosphere in the room was tense. Cyrus stood by the window, his eyes glistening with unshed tears as he gazed out at the shadowy village.

Jake noticed the silence from Cyrus and walked over. "You alright, man?" Jake asked softly. "You've been really quiet."

Cyrus exhaled; his breath shaky. "It's just... I've been thinking about my uncle, Alfred Dusk. He used to tell me stories about Ebonvale, stories about the good days, before all the mysteries and dangers swallowed this place." His voice cracked. "He always knew something was wrong, but he never got the chance to do anything about it."

Jake placed a comforting hand on his friend's shoulder. "We're going to solve this, Cyrus. For your uncle, for Finnian, for everyone in Ebonvale."

Just as Jake spoke, they all remembered they hadn't asked Finnian about his disappearance. Evelyn, who had been quiet so far, turned to Finnian. "Finnian, we haven't asked... how did you end up in the woods? Did you see anyone or remember anything?"

Finnian frowned; the memory foggy but unsettling. "When we were in that house, Jake held my hand... but then I saw something out of the corner of my eye, in the room next to us. I don't know why, but I pulled my hand free and went inside to check. I thought I'd call you all... but before I could, someone hit me from behind. Just before I blacked out, I noticed mining equipment—new tools, not old, dusty ones. Miners' clothes were hanging there too. I woke up in the forest, and then you found me."

Evelyn's eyes widened. "New mining tools? But that place was supposed to be abandoned..."

"The note they left near Finnian was for someone else," Cyrus added, his tone dark. "Whoever this is, they're getting desperate. This kidnapping was their last warning."

Jake nodded, determination in his gaze. "We'll face whatever comes. Tomorrow night, we'll find out what they've been hiding."

CHAPTER SIXTEEN

The Mayor's Deceit: The Coal Conspiracy

The next day, the group roamed the village, the weight of their mission bearing down on them. The Lantern Festival was in full swing, but none of them could shake the feeling that something dark lurked beneath the surface of Ebonvale. They decided to visit Old Man Grayson.

As they approached his house, there he was, as usual, standing outside, casually puffing on a cigar. His gaze was distant, fixed on the haunted thicket behind his home.

"Well, well, my favourite bunch," Grayson greeted them with a warm smile. "What brings you lot here?"

Cyrus exchanged a glance with the others. They decided not to mention the shortcut path that led to Grayson's backyard. Instead, they sat and talked casually, knowing deep down they could trust him. There was no reason to doubt Grayson, who had always been a kind and trustworthy figure in Ebonvale. If anything, the person behind the conspiracy had chosen his backyard for that very reason—to use his unsuspecting nature as a cover.

The conversation flowed easily, Grayson reminiscing about old times while the group, careful not to reveal too much, observed for any signs of suspicion. But Grayson was as he always was—an open book, seemingly unaware of the dark undercurrents surrounding him.

When they left, Cyrus whispered to Jake, "It makes sense. Whoever's behind all this used Grayson's property because no one would ever suspect him. It's the perfect cover."

As night fell, the group gathered at the edge of Forsaken Hall, the old town hall that had been abandoned for years. Shadows stretched long across the village, and the only sound was the distant hum of the festival in the village square.

They took their positions, hiding near a cracked window to observe what would happen. The air was heavy with dread.

Moments later, Mayor Finch arrived, his face twisted with anger. He began pacing, muttering to himself in frustration. "Those kids... they're getting too close," he growled.

Then, a second figure entered—the tall, imposing form of Anklov Welles, Orion's assistant. Finch's fury erupted. He stormed over to Anklov, grabbing him by the collar.

"You fool!" Finch snarled. "You can't even handle four kids, and you think you can run an operation like this? Do you even realize what would've happened if I hadn't been there at the Forsaken Woods' house to knock that kid out? They would've found everything—everything, Anklov! What if I hadn't been there on time at the so-called haunted house, which isn't haunted at all? What if I hadn't hit Finnian when I did?" Finch's voice grew more furious with each word. "They would've seen the miners extracting coal from under the tunnel of that house. We would've been exposed—caught! And what if the boss had found out? We'd have been finished right there, yesterday, you fool!"

Anklov stammered, "I—I'm sorry, Mayor. I..."

"The fourth truck leaves tomorrow from Misttvale Crossing," Finch spat. "If anything goes wrong, the boss will have both our heads."

The group, hidden behind the window, exchanged horrified glances. They had uncovered more than they could have ever imagined. Illegal coal mining, trucks smuggling out the coal, and Mayor Finch was behind it all. But the worst part was yet to come.

As the realization sunk in, Cyrus's mind raced. He thought back to the tunnels they had stumbled upon earlier. There had been two exits, but neither seemed large enough to be used for smuggling coal out in large quantities. Both exits were narrow and didn't seem equipped for anything beyond foot traffic or small tools. And yet, now it was clear: Finch's operation had been going on for years. How had they missed it?

Then it clicked.

Outside the tunnels, near the entrance in the Forsaken Woods, they had spotted several old mine carts, rusted and worn, but still functional. At the time, they hadn't paid them much attention, assuming they were remnants from a time long past. But now, it made sense. Those mine carts were being used to extract the coal under the cover of darkness. Finch's men had likely been using the carts to transport the coal through hidden pathways they hadn't yet uncovered.

"We missed something," Cyrus whispered, barely audible as he crouched lower behind the window. "The exits we saw...they weren't the real ones. There has to be another way they're getting the coal out. The carts outside—"

Jake nodded; his eyes wide with realization. "They're using those mine carts to move the coal out of here, probably through a hidden tunnel we haven't found yet."

Evelyn looked back toward the dark trees outside, her mind racing. "So, the real exit... it could be deeper in the Forsaken Woods or somewhere we haven't looked. And they've been covering it up this whole time."

The group now understands there's a hidden method Finch and his team have been using to transport coal, and the next part of their mission will be to find that secret route.

Suddenly a third figure stepped into the hall; his face hidden by the shadows. The air thickened with tension. The group tried to make out who it was, but he stayed in the dark. His voice, however, was unmistakable.

"I don't care what it takes," the man said, his tone cold and authoritative. "The truck leaves tomorrow. And if you fail again, neither of you will survive to see the end of this operation."

Jake's eyes widened. "I think...That voice... it's him... Orion Wellesley. It has to be."

The group's suspicions now pointed squarely at Orion, especially with his assistant involved. But was Orion the mastermind? And what was this boss they kept referring to?

The group slipped away from the forsaken hall, hearts still pounding from the revelations they had overheard. The night air was cool, but the weight of what they had just uncovered felt suffocating. As they moved through the narrow streets of Ebonvale, the question loomed: who was the mastermind behind Mayor Finch and Anklov? And what deeper secrets still lay hidden beneath the village?

"We can't wait until tomorrow," Cyrus said, his voice low but urgent as they reached the edge of the village. "That truck leaves at Misttvale Crossing tomorrow evening. If we don't find where those tunnels lead tonight, we'll miss our chance."

Finnian nodded, still pale from his ordeal. "We can't let them get away with this. Not again."

Jake, always the first to spring into action, smacked his fist into his palm. "Alright, so we go back. To the tunnels. We missed something last time."

"Back?" Evelyn's eyes widened, her voice trembling slightly. "You mean... back to the tunnel under the stone?"

"Yes," Cyrus replied, his jaw set. "We don't have a choice. We need to figure out where those tunnels lead—and we need to do it now."

The group hurried toward Misttvale Crossing, the wind swirling around them, carrying the distant sound of rustling leaves and creaking branches. The thick fog seemed to part just enough to allow their passage, as if the shadows themselves were guiding them back to the source of the village's darkness.

They arrived at the familiar stone at the edge of the thicket, the very one they had uncovered weeks ago. The stone sat heavy and unmoving, just as they had left it.

"This is it," Cyrus whispered. His lantern flickered in his hand, casting long, eerie shadows on the forest floor. "Under here is where it all started."

Jake knelt down beside the stone, his eyes scanning the ground. "Last time, we didn't go deep enough. There's more to this tunnel system than we thought."

Finnian hesitated. "What if we get lost down there? It's not exactly a safe place, and now we know these tunnels are used for... illegal things."

"We won't get lost," Cyrus said with firm determination. "We don't have a choice. We have to stop them."

With a collective breath, the group set to work, carefully shifting the stone aside to reveal the dark, gaping mouth of the tunnel beneath. One by one, they descended into the underground, their footsteps echoing faintly against the cold, damp stone.

The darkness swallowed them whole, and the air grew colder, more oppressive with each step they took. Their lanterns barely pierced the thick blackness that stretched endlessly before them.

"Do you feel that?" Evelyn's voice was barely a whisper, yet it trembled with fear. "It's... like something's watching us."

"We're not alone down here," Finnian murmured. "There's something—"

"Shh," Cyrus hushed him, his eyes focused ahead. "There's something up ahead."

They pressed on, their lanterns illuminating a winding pathway that twisted and turned, deeper into the earth. As they went, they noticed strange markings etched into the stone walls—symbols that seemed old, far older than anything they had seen in Ebonvale before. Evelyn squinted at one of the symbols, her heart skipping a beat.

"I've seen this before," she muttered.

Cyrus stopped and glanced back. "What do you mean?"

Evelyn stepped closer to the wall, tracing the symbol with her finger. It was faint but unmistakable—a swirling design like the one she had seen carved into the tree in the thicket where they had found the coal. "This symbol... it was on that old tree near the clearing. Victor Valtor's ghost showed me this mark. I think it's a marker, like a signpost. Maybe... one of these tunnels leads out near there."

"That tree?" Jake's brow furrowed. "Where we found that coal scattered on the ground?"

Finnian nodded. "Exactly. It's like someone marked the path, or maybe it's meant to help them navigate through the tunnels."

"Then one of the exits might be closer than we thought," Cyrus said, his eyes glinting with a renewed sense of purpose. "This symbol could be the key."

The air grew thicker, more difficult to breathe, and an overwhelming sense of dread settled in their chests as they continued along the tunnel, the symbols seeming to guide their path.

Finally, they reached a massive iron gate embedded in the stone, its surface rusted and worn with age. Beyond it, the tunnel continued—but now, something was different. The ground sloped downward, revealing a faintly glowing pit further ahead.

"What is that?" Jake muttered.

Cyrus stepped closer, peering through the gaps in the gate. "It's... a mine cart."

"A mine cart?" Finnian exclaimed. "But where's the exit? We know they're smuggling coal out of these tunnels, but we didn't see an obvious way out last time."

"That's because the exit's hidden," Cyrus said grimly. "Look."

Beyond the pit lay tracks, disappearing into the darkness on the other side. A few old mine carts were lined up along the tracks, still faintly gleaming with coal dust. One of the carts looked newer, cleaner—recently used.

"They've been using this," Cyrus said, his voice low. "This is where they're transporting the coal, out of this tunnel. But where does it lead?"

Jake crouched down, inspecting the tracks closely. "There's a slope going deeper into the ground. It must lead under the thicket, maybe all the way to the village outskirts or beyond."

"But how do they get the coal out without anyone noticing?" Evelyn asked, her voice tinged with panic. "Where does it come out on the other side?"

"We missed something last time," Finnian said. "This tunnel connects somewhere above ground. A place unseen or forgotten by Ebonvale. That's how they're moving the coal without anyone seeing."

Jake straightened, his jaw tight. "We need to follow this path. All the way."

Evelyn hesitated. "Are we sure we want to know where it leads?"

Cyrus nodded, his face set in grim determination. "We have to. If we don't, they'll get away with it—just like they did eighteen years ago when Uncle Alfred disappeared."

With that, they pressed onward, following the narrow tracks deeper into the tunnel. The mine carts rattled faintly as they moved past, the rails leading further and further into the bowels of Ebonvale. The air was thick with dust, and the eerie glow from the pit cast unsettling shadows on the walls.

As they reached the end of the tunnel, they found themselves at the base of a steep, stone staircase leading upward, towards the surface.

"Do you think this is it?" Finnian asked, his voice barely above a whisper. "The exit?"

"There's only one way to find out," Cyrus said, gripping his lantern tightly as he began to ascend the steps. The others followed close behind, their hearts racing as they climbed higher

and higher.

CHAPTER SEVENTEEN

The Coal Conspiracy: Unravelling Ebonvale's Darkness

When they finally emerged from the tunnel, they found themselves in a small, dense patch of trees—a tiny forest-like area that seemed secluded and untouched. The air here felt colder, heavier, as if the surrounding nature itself was burdened by some ancient curse. As they cautiously moved forward, the trees began to thin, and a vast, still body of water appeared before them.

"Blackwater Lake..." Finnian whispered, recognizing it instantly. The lake's surface was dark—too dark. It seemed to swallow the moonlight, casting a blackish, almost oily sheen over the water. There were no ripples, no sound of wildlife, only an eerie silence that made their skin crawl.

"I've heard about this place," Finnian continued, his voice low and tense. "Grayson told me no one ever comes here... it's haunted."

The rest of the group exchanged uneasy glances. Blackwater Lake had long been considered a cursed spot in Ebonvale. Tales of disappearances, strange apparitions, and unsettling noises had kept the villagers far away for generations. But now, standing at its shore, they realized why no one ever came near. The lake felt wrong—like a portal to something dark and malevolent.

"They've been using this lake," Jake said, scanning the area with narrowed eyes. "Transporting coal through here to Forsaken Woods. No one would ever come close enough to notice."

Cyrus nodded grimly. "That's how they've been hiding it. They've turned a cursed place into a smuggler's paradise. But if Anklov was coming from here the night we saw him... that means they're still moving coal, probably through this exact route."

As they walked further, the tension in the air thickened. The mist rolling off the lake twisted in unnatural ways, curling around their feet like ghostly fingers. Every step felt heavy, as if unseen eyes were watching them from the shadows.

Suddenly, a faint sound echoed from the lake—a low, mournful moan that sent a chill racing down their spines.

"What was that?" Evelyn gasped, gripping Jake's arm.

"Could be the wind," Jake muttered, though his voice lacked conviction.

But as they stood frozen, listening, the moan came again—closer this time. The surface of the lake remained still, but the sound was undeniable, as if something—something unseen—was lurking just beneath the black water.

"We need to keep moving," Cyrus urged, though even he sounded rattled.

They quickened their pace, leaving the lake behind, but the feeling of dread stayed with them, clinging like the mist. Every now and then, the wind would carry a distant whisper, unintelligible but filled with malice, as if the lake was calling them back.

Finally, after what felt like an eternity, they reached the edge of Forsaken Woods. The trees here were gnarled and twisted, their branches like skeletal arms reaching toward the sky. It was the same spot they had been two nights ago when they saw Anklov emerge from the woods. Now it all made sense—he had been coming from Blackwater Lake, likely after overseeing the departure of another truckload of coal.

Cyrus gestured toward the woods. "This is it. Anklov was here... and now, so are we."

Finnian swallowed hard, his eyes scanning the treeline. "But Forsaken Woods... it's different. Grayson said this place was really haunted."

"Haunted or not, we have to go in," Cyrus said, his voice low but resolute. "We're running out of time."

As they stared into the dark mouth of Forsaken Woods, a cold wind swept through the trees, carrying with it the faint sound of distant whispers, like voices long forgotten. The shadows between the trees shifted unnaturally, as if something was moving within, just beyond sight.

They had no choice now. The truth awaited them somewhere in the depths of Forsaken Woods. But so did something else—something much darker.

With one last glance at each other, the group took a deep breath and stepped into the forest, knowing full well they might not be alone.

As the group stepped into Forsaken Woods, the towering trees casting twisted shadows in the dim moonlight. The woods were eerily silent, as if they were holding their breath, waiting for something terrible to unfold. The air was thick with tension, every snap of a twig beneath their boots sending shivers down their spines. This time, there would be no distractions. This time, they were determined to unearth the truth.

"We missed something last time," Cyrus muttered, his lantern casting flickering shadows on the dense foliage. "This is where Finch led us astray, but not this time. We need to keep going."

With a collective nod, the group pressed deeper into the forest, retracing their steps. Soon, they reached the familiar chamber—the hidden entryway where they had followed Anklov before. It felt strangely vacant now, as if the spirits that had once haunted them were lying in wait, observing silently. The tunnel before them yawned open, cold and unwelcoming, but the group steeled themselves and moved forward.

The tunnel twisted and turned, the walls damp and slick with moisture. Unlike before, there were no ghosts, no shadows flitting through the darkness—just the oppressive silence of the underground passage.

"It's too quiet," Evelyn whispered, her eyes darting around nervously. "No shadows, no spirits..."

"They've done their part," Cyrus replied, his voice steady. "Whatever haunted this place, they've led us here for a reason. We're close now."

At the end of the tunnel, they climbed the steps, emerging once again into the clearing near the abandoned house—the same house where they had lost Finnian last time. The decaying structure loomed before them, its wooden beams creaking softly in the night breeze. The house felt even more sinister now, a dark relic of Ebonvale's buried past.

"This place..." Jake muttered, staring at the dilapidated walls. "This is where everything connects."

"This time," Finnian said, determination hardening his voice, "we're going to find out what's been hidden here."

The group moved cautiously toward the house, their footsteps muffled by the overgrown grass and fallen leaves. As they stepped inside, the familiar musty air greeted them, thick with the stench of decay and forgotten memories. Without hesitation, they headed straight for the room where Finnian had blacked out the last time—the place where they had first glimpsed the truth.

The room was cluttered with old miner's uniforms, rusted tools, and a few broken lanterns. The sight of them sent a chill through Finnian. He had seen these things before, but this time, they felt more ominous, more significant. Something was off.

"They used to mine here," Finnian said, picking up an old, dusty pickaxe. "But why in this house?"

Cyrus scanned the room, frustration etched on his face. "There's got to be more. We're missing something."

As they searched the room, moving through old debris and forgotten relics, Evelyn suddenly froze, her eyes widening. "Look!"

They turned just in time to see the same ghostly woman who had once grabbed Jake's hand. She moved quickly, gliding across the room without making a sound, her pale figure disappearing into one of the adjacent rooms.

"Follow her!" Cyrus shouted, running after her, the rest of the group close behind.

They rushed into the room where the ghost had vanished, but it was empty—nothing but dust and silence. The ghost was gone, but something was definitely hidden here. They searched frantically, and just as the quiet settled over them, a strange noise echoed beneath their feet—a faint rumbling, as if something was moving underground.

Finnian's heart raced as he bent down, pressing his ear to the floor. "There's something beneath us..."

Before he could finish, Cyrus noticed a wooden board that had come loose. He quickly pulled at it, revealing a small, narrow entrance beneath the floorboards.

"There!" Cyrus exclaimed. "This is what we've been looking for."

With renewed determination, the group descended into the hidden passage, squeezing through the narrow space until they landed behind a heavy stone wall. They crouched low, their hearts pounding as they peered around the corner—and what they saw left them breathless.

There, in the cavernous underground space, 10 to 15 miners worked relentlessly, chipping away at the rock. The area was a mining site, coal being extracted and loaded into mine carts.

Unlike the carts they had seen before, these were fitted to run on tracks that snaked through the underground. It was an entire hidden operation, concealed beneath the town's haunted facade.

"This is it," Jake whispered, his voice barely audible. "This is where they've been mining all along."

"Look at the tracks," Finnian muttered, pointing toward the rails that led deeper into the tunnel. "These aren't just for underground—they're connected to something bigger."

The group silently followed the tracks, carefully ducking behind rocks and abandoned equipment, their breath tight in their chests. The tracks led them further into the tunnel until they reached an opening—the Echoing Hollow. There, the tracks came to an abrupt end, but not without a clear sign of what had been happening.

Coal-filled carts, with wheels designed to run on roads, were lined up near the hollow. One path from the hollow led to Blackwater Lake, the other led back toward Misttvale Crossing.

"That's how they've been transporting it," Cyrus whispered, realization dawning on him. "Through these tunnels, they load the coal into road carts and move it out. They've been using these paths for years without anyone noticing."

"They've kept it hidden with all the ghost stories and rumors," Jake added. "No one would ever come near these places. It's genius."

"And look," Evelyn pointed, her voice filled with tension. "The trucks—they're getting ready to depart."

They turned and saw the dim outlines of trucks parked near the exit. Tomorrow evening, the coal would be on its way out of Ebonvale—unless they stopped it.

"We have to tell the sheriff," Finnian said, urgency creeping into his voice. "This is it. This is the proof we need."

Cyrus nodded, his eyes set with grim determination. "Let's get out of here."

Retracing their steps, they followed the second path out of the tunnels, emerging at Misttvale Crossing. This exit was hidden, separate from the secret tunnel they had uncovered beneath the stone.

Breathing heavily, they made their way to the sheriff's office, their footsteps quickening as the enormity of what they had uncovered weighed on their minds.

Bursts of adrenaline fueled them as they reached the sheriff. Bursting through the doors, Cyrus spoke first, his voice firm and urgent. "We have everything. The coal, the trucks, the tunnels—it's all there. Tomorrow evening, they're planning to move the trucks. You need to stop them."

The sheriff listened intently, his eyes widening as the group laid out the conspiracy that had festered beneath Ebonvale for years. The weight of the town's dark history had finally come to light—and tomorrow, they would bring it to an end.

CHAPTER EIGHTEEN

Fading Shadows: Ebonvale's Redemption Unveiled

The group awoke the next morning feeling lighter than they had in days. After so many unanswered questions, so much darkness hovering over Ebonvale, they finally saw a glimmer of hope. Finnian and Cyrus, along with Evelyn and Jake, were filled with anticipation. That evening, everything would come to light. They would reveal the truth to the world, and Ebonvale's long history of deceit and death would finally end.

Just before sunset, they met with Sheriff Malcom, leading him and his team of officers to the secret tunnels and hidden paths they'd uncovered. They showed the skeletons they found—the haunting remains in the Forsaken Hall, including Mark Blackwood's bones and the skeleton buried beneath the abandoned house in Forsaken Woods. As the sheriff's team carefully collected the remains for further investigation, there was a silent understanding that these long-forgotten souls were finally on their way to justice. Each step the group took felt heavier as the weight of these past atrocities became real to them. They had to move quickly, quietly, ensuring that Mayor Finch and his accomplices remained unaware of their discovery.

The real goal was to catch the one they suspected was pulling the strings—Orion Wellesley. The group was sure that tonight would bring everything to a close.

By evening, the sheriff, his officers, and the group were in position, hiding at Misttvale Crossing, where the truck loaded with illegal coal was about to make its departure. The atmosphere was tense, filled with expectation. Shadows deepened as the sun sank, and the workers loaded the truck, completely unaware of the trap set for them.

As the final crates were loaded, Sheriff Malcom signaled his team. They stepped out of their hiding places, surrounding the workers. "Hands in the air!" the sheriff ordered.

Panic set in, but the workers, seeing the law surrounding them, quickly surrendered. A few moments of harsh questioning by the sheriff revealed what the group had expected: Mayor Finch and Anklov were at the center of this operation. However, the workers didn't seem to know the real mastermind, the one behind it all.

Within hours, news spread through Ebonvale like wildfire. The once-respected mayor was a criminal, and Orion's assistant, Anklov, was involved in a conspiracy that had claimed lives and destroyed families for over two decades. The villagers whispered in fear and disbelief. Could it be true? Could the village's leaders, the ones they had trusted for so long, be responsible for such horrors?

Soon after capturing the truck, Sheriff Malcom moved swiftly, arresting both Mayor Finch and Anklov from their homes. The mayor's pleas rang through the night as he was dragged from his residence. "You've got it all wrong!" Finch yelled, turning to the group. "I did it for the good of the town! You have to believe me! This isn't what it looks like!"

Anklov, ever composed, stared straight at the group as he was handcuffed. "We were building a future," he muttered coldly, his eyes locking with Finnian's. "You should have stayed out of it."

The group, standing beside the sheriff, watched them both being taken away. But something didn't feel right. Despite their capture, they knew that Mayor Finch and Anklov weren't the true masterminds. There was someone else. Someone more dangerous.

The real boss was still out there.

The sheriff, knowing the group had uncovered more than anyone else could, took Mayor Finch into the station for a long, grueling interrogation. As hours passed, tension mounted. Finnian, Cyrus, Evelyn, and Jake waited outside the police station, pacing anxiously. Each minute felt like a lifetime.

When Sheriff Malcom finally emerged, his face was a mix of exhaustion and disbelief. The group rushed toward him. "Who was it?" Cyrus asked breathlessly. "Who's behind all this?"

The sheriff sighed, glancing at the ground for a moment before looking them in the eye. "We're going to bring him in. You'll get to see for yourselves."

The group exchanged looks, hearts pounding in their chests. They were certain it was Orion.

But when the sheriff's team returned, it wasn't Orion in handcuffs. It was Old Man Grayson.

For a moment, time stood still. The group's eyes widened, unable to comprehend what they were seeing. Grayson—kind, gruff Grayson, the man they had trusted—stood there, looking broken and defeated. The man who had helped them, who had seemed to be on their side all along, was the mastermind behind everything.

"Grayson?" Finnian whispered, his voice trembling with disbelief. "Why?"

Tears welled up in Evelyn's eyes as she stepped forward, confronting the old man. "You... You were with us the whole time. Why would you do this?"

Grayson looked at them, his eyes filled with regret, but also something cold, something dark that had been buried deep within him for years. "I didn't want to kill you," he said softly. "Not you boys... not after what I did to your uncle."

The revelation hit Cyrus and Finnian like a physical blow. Their uncle, Alfred Dusk, the man they had looked up to all their lives, had been murdered—by Grayson.

The sheriff's interrogation of Grayson was brutal, but the old man answered each question without hesitation. His confessions were like a hammer driving nails into the group's hearts.

"When did it all start?" the sheriff asked, pacing the room, his voice cold.

"Twenty-five years ago," Grayson began, his voice raspy with emotion. "The government banned the coal mine, said it was too dangerous to continue. But I saw an opportunity. Twenty-two years ago, I started it all—the illegal mining."

"And the tourists?" Sheriff Malcom pressed, his tone sharp. "The ones who disappeared twenty years ago?"

Grayson's face darkened. "They found the tunnel at Misttvale Crossing... they were going to expose us. We couldn't let that happen. So, we killed them. Buried their bodies in the Forsaken Hall."

The room felt suffocating. The air heavy with the weight of his confession.

"What about Mark Blackwood? Why keep him alive?"

Grayson's lips twisted into a bitter smile. "He was supposed to be one of us. But when we found out he was gathering evidence against us, we had no choice. We killed him and buried his body in Echoing Hollow."

"And Victor Valtor?" the sheriff continued. "What about him?"

Grayson's eyes flickered with guilt. "Victor escaped, tried to go to Mayor Finch. But the mayor was with us. We killed him in Forsaken Woods, left his body as a warning."

"Were all the ghost sightings just your men in disguise?" Sheriff Malcom asked, leaning in.

Grayson shook his head. "Some were. But others... others were real. The ghosts of those tourists... they're still out there, haunting Ebonvale."

The final question hung in the air, heavier than all the rest. Finnian stepped forward, his voice trembling. "Why... why didn't you kill us? You had so many chances. Why did you let us live?"

Grayson's voice cracked with emotion. "Because of your uncle. Alfred Dusk was one of my closest friends, before all this. I killed him with my own hands, and I've regretted it every day since. When you boys showed up, I couldn't bring myself to do it. Not after what I'd done to your family."

"And why did you kill our uncle?" Cyrus whispered, his throat tight with emotion.

Grayson's eyes filled with tears. "Alfred was close to figuring it all out. He thought Finch was the mastermind, and he trusted me. He told me everything. I led him to Blackwater Lake, offered him a partnership... but he refused. So I... I had to kill him."

The group stood in stunned silence as the full weight of the truth settled over them.

The next day, with heavy hearts, they gathered at Blackwater Lake. Grayson had led them to the spot where Alfred Dusk was buried, and after digging for what felt like hours, they uncovered his body. Tears streamed down Cyrus and Finnian's faces as they knelt beside their uncle's grave, mourning the man who had been taken from them.

In a sombre ceremony, the sheriff, his team, the group, and the families of those lost over the years laid to rest the bodies of Alfred Dusk, Victor Valtor, Mark Blackwood, and the forgotten tourists.

The group was quiet as they returned to Cyrus's house after the ceremony. The weight of the day hung heavy on their hearts. They had given proper burials to the forgotten souls of Ebonvale—Alfred Dusk, Victor Valtor, Mark Blackwood, and the missing tourists—but it still didn't feel like closure. The shadows of their discoveries loomed large, and the ghosts of the past lingered in their minds.

Evelyn, Jake, Finnian, and Cyrus sat around the dimly lit room, each lost in their own thoughts. The fire crackled softly, but it did little to ease the somber mood. As the hours wore on and night settled in, they decided to spend the night together, too emotionally drained to part ways.

Suddenly, there was a knock on the door.

Cyrus froze, the familiar sense of déjà vu washing over him. He stood up slowly and opened the door, but no one was there. The night air was still, and all he could see was a faint shadow moving toward the edge of the village, slipping into the thicket.

His heart raced as recognition dawned on him. "It's the same shadow," he whispered, his voice barely audible. He turned back to the others. "The one I saw that night, leading us to Misttvale Crossing."

The group exchanged wary glances but quickly followed Cyrus, determination overriding their fear. The shadow led them through the winding paths of Ebonvale, deeper into the heart of the night. The village lights faded into the distance as they crossed the familiar paths toward the Blackwater Lake.

As they reached the lake, the shadow stopped, standing just at the water's edge. The group halted, breathless and tense. The shadow was hard to make out in the darkness, but something about it felt familiar, especially to Cyrus and Finnian.

The figure moved closer, and as the moonlight glinted off the still waters of the lake, the shadow began to take form. Finnian's breath caught in his throat.

"Uncle Alfred..." he whispered.

The shadow became clearer, and there before them stood the ghost of Alfred Dusk.

Cyrus and Finnian's hearts swelled with emotion. Alfred's spectral form was as familiar as it was surreal, and though his face was calm, his eyes seemed to carry years of untold stories. He stepped forward, and his voice, though ethereal, was steady.

"I've always been with you," Alfred said softly, his gaze drifting between Cyrus and Finnian. "Not just me. All of us."

The group looked around as one by one, more shadows began to appear—Victor Valtor, Mark Blackwood, and the ghosts of the tourists who had been lost in the tragedies of Ebonvale. The air was thick with the presence of the past.

Finnian blinked in disbelief. "All this time, you've been helping us?"

Alfred nodded. "When I led you to Misttvale Crossing, I showed you the hidden tunnel. Victor showed you the mark on the tree and the coal. Mark Blackwood revealed the tunnel under Echoing Hollow. And the hand that guided Jake in Echoing Hollow—that was Mark too. Every step you took, we were there, helping you uncover the truth."

Evelyn's eyes widened as she recalled their journey. "The woman's ghost in the abandoned house... she led us to the hidden tunnel there."

"Yes," Alfred said. "The real ghosts of Ebonvale have been with you since the beginning. You were never alone. We couldn't rest until the truth was brought to light."

The realization struck the group like a wave. All along, they had believed they were being hunted by the ghosts of Ebonvale, but in reality, those very spirits had been guiding them, watching over them, helping them piece together the secrets buried deep within the village's history.

Cyrus's voice trembled as he spoke, his heart full. "Why did you stay? Why did you help us?"

Alfred looked at him, a sad smile on his face. "Because you are family, Cyrus. You and Finnian. I could never let the two of you fall into the same darkness that claimed me. And those who were wronged in Ebonvale... they needed their story to be told."

Tears welled in Finnian's eyes. "But now...?"

"Our work is done," Alfred replied, his voice tinged with a bittersweet note. "We can finally rest. The truth has been revealed, and Ebonvale will heal."

One by one, the ghosts began to fade, their forms shimmering in the moonlight. The group, overwhelmed with emotion, bowed their heads in gratitude, paying silent respect to the spirits who had unknowingly become their allies.

With heavy hearts, the group said their final goodbyes. Alfred was the last to fade, his gaze lingering on Cyrus and Finnian for a moment longer.

“Goodbye,” Alfred whispered. “Remember, you’re never truly alone. Even in the darkest times, light will find its way.”

As Alfred’s spirit disappeared into the night, Cyrus stood silently, staring at the place where his uncle had been moments before. The night felt still, but also lighter—like a weight had been lifted from the air around them.

The group stood together in silence, the enormity of everything they had been through settling into their hearts.

Finally, Cyrus spoke, his voice calm but resolute.

“We thought we were chasing shadows, trying to solve the mysteries of the past. But in the end, the shadows were guiding us toward the truth. And now, those shadows can rest.”

The group looked up at him, the words sinking in.

“In Ebonvale,” Cyrus continued, “secrets may be buried, but the truth... the truth always finds a way to rise.”

And with that, the chapter of their journey came to a close, leaving behind a village forever changed—by the past and by the courage of those willing to uncover it.

THE END

Epilogue

Months had passed since the events that had forever changed Ebonvale. The once-shrouded village was no longer cloaked in the fog of secrecy. Word of the illegal mining operation, the murders, and the buried truths spread far and wide. Ebonvale, once a place of whispered rumors and hidden shadows, was finally at peace, its dark past laid bare.

Cyrus and Finnian returned to their daily lives, but they knew they would never see the world the same way again. The journey had marked them, left them changed. They had unearthed not just the physical remains of the past but the emotional weight of generations haunted by their silence. The brothers often found themselves standing at the edge of the lake, remembering the final goodbye from the spirits who had helped guide them. The village was at peace now, and so were the souls of those long forgotten.

Evelyn and Jake, too, carried with them the memories of the trials they had faced. The horrors they had witnessed, the bravery they had summoned—it was now part of who they were. The bonds between the four were stronger than ever, forged in the crucible of shared terror and triumph.

But Ebonvale was still Ebonvale. There were scars that would never fully heal—old wounds that the village would carry for years to come. While the ghosts were at rest, the memories of what had been uncovered would linger. And in the stillness of certain nights, when the wind swept across the forsaken woods, one might still hear faint whispers. Whispers of those who had lived and died there. Whispers of the courage of four people who dared to confront the darkness head-on.

For Finnian, Cyrus, Evelyn, and Jake, Ebonvale would always be more than just their home. It was a place of secrets—both buried and brought to light. But most of all, it was a place that reminded them of one undeniable truth: sometimes the past must be faced, no matter how terrifying, in order to find peace.

As they moved forward, they knew one thing for certain: Ebonvale would never be the same. It was finally free, and so were they.

Author's Note

As I sit here reflecting on the journey that brought this story to life, I am overwhelmed with a sense of gratitude and wonder. Ebonvale: Shadows of Secrets began as a whisper of an idea, a tale of mystery and courage, but it has become something far more meaningful to me than just words on a page. It is a story about confronting the unknown, about the bravery it takes to uncover the truth—even when that truth is painful. It is about finding light in the darkest corners and realizing that even the most haunted places can be healed through perseverance and hope.

To my readers, I want to say thank you. Thank you for trusting me to guide you through the shadows of Ebonvale, for following these characters and their journey through fear, heartbreak, and discovery. Each of you brought this story to life in your own way, and for that, I am deeply thankful.

Writing this book has been a labor of love, and every moment spent crafting its twists and turns has been made worthwhile knowing that it found its way into your hands. If there's one thing I hope you take away from this story, it's that even in the face of the unknown, there's always a way forward, always a truth waiting to be uncovered. And that we are never truly alone on this path, whether in life or in fiction.

To my family and friends—your unwavering support and encouragement carried me through the highs and lows of this creative process. To my dad, who believed in me even when I doubted myself—you are the heart behind this book. And to everyone who has been part of this journey, whether through kind words, inspiration, or simply being present—I am forever grateful.

Thank you for being part of this adventure.

Sincerely,

Utakarsh Singh

www.ingramcontent.com/pod-product-compliance
Lightning Source LLC
LaVergne TN
LVHW041113150826
845673LV00007B/2032